A Deep Dark Secret

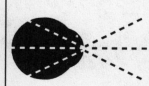

This Large Print Book carries the
Seal of Approval of N.A.V.H.

A Deep Dark Secret

Kimberla Lawson Roby

THORNDIKE PRESS
A part of Gale, Cengage Learning

GALE
CENGAGE Learning™

Detroit • New York • San Francisco • New Haven, Conn • Waterville, Maine • London

GALE
CENGAGE Learning™

LIBRARY OF CONGRESS CATALOGING-IN-PUBLICATION DATA

Roby, Kimberla Lawson.
  A deep dark secret / by Kimberla Lawson Roby.
    p. cm. — (Thorndike Press large print African-American)
  ISBN-13: 978-1-4104-2408-2 (alk. paper)
  ISBN-10: 1-4104-2408-1 (alk. paper)
  1. Sexually abused girls—Fiction. 2. Stepfathers—Fiction. 3.
Deacons—Fiction. 4. Large type books. I. Title.
PS3568.O3189D44 2010
813'.54—dc22   2009052082

Published in 2010 by arrangement with William Morrow, an imprint of
HarperCollins Publishers.

Printed in the United States of America
1 2 3 4 5 6 7 14 13 12 11 10

For every woman, man,
or child who holds a deep
dark childhood secret

ACKNOWLEDGMENTS

To God for all the countless blessings you have given my family and me and for your unwavering guidance.

To my heart and joy — my husband, Will. I love you so very much, and thank you for everything.

Much love to my wonderful brothers, Willie Jr. and Michael Stapleton, and the rest of my loving family members (I always end up leaving out someone, so I won't list every name, but if you share the same bloodline as I do or the same bloodline as Will does, then you are the family members I'm talking about!); my first cousin, Patricia Haley, who I grew up side by side with the same as if we were sisters; the women who are more like sisters than friends: Kelli Bullard, Lori Thurman, Janell Green, and Victoria Christopher Murray; and my writer friends: E. Lynn Harris, Trisha R. Thomas, Eric Jerome Dickey, Mary B. Morrison, Eric

Pete, Cheryl Robinson, Lolita Files, and Re-Shonda Tate Billingsley.

To my amazing assistant, Connie Dettman; my incredible agent, Elaine Koster; my new editor, Carrie Feron, for such great advice on this novella; my very supportive publisher, William Morrow/Avon; every bookseller and retailer that sells my books; and all the people in radio, TV, and print who publicize my work to the masses. Thank you for all that you've done for me for so many years now.

Then, last but certainly not least, to my very caring and very loyal readers — thank you for all the love and support you always give and know that I love each of you from the very bottom of my soul.

Much love and God bless you always,
Kimberla Lawson Roby

PROLOGUE

Jillian Maxwell finished her nightly talk with God, climbed into bed, and knew for sure that she was the luckiest seven-year-old in the world. It was the reason that, even though her eyes were now closed and she was snuggling into a very comfortable sleeping position, she couldn't stop smiling. She'd never been happier, and just the thought of how her life had changed so miraculously over the last two years made her excited. She was excited because she finally had the one thing she'd always wanted. She finally had the best thing any girl could hope for. She finally had a father.

And what a truly wonderful and very loving man he was. He loved her mommy, he loved her, and he went out of his way to make sure they had everything they needed. As a matter of fact, ever since he'd come into their lives, not once had she heard her mommy talking about bills, money, or the idea that she needed to find a better job. Not once had Jillian had to wait until payday to get new clothes, shoes, or any of the other things she sometimes needed, or even certain things she occasionally wanted. Her father took care of them completely and had made it clear from the very start that he didn't want Jillian thinking of him as just some stepfather. He'd told her that while sadly he wasn't her biological father, he already loved her like she was his own and would be honored if she would call him Daddy. Jillian still remembered the warm feeling she'd felt the day he'd sat her down to have this particular conversation and how pleased her mommy had been as well. Her mommy had even shed a few tears of joy, and there had been no question in either of their minds that Byron James was the answer to both their prayers.

Then, believe it or not, today, life had gotten even better for them, because as of 6:40 this morning, Jillian now had a beautiful little baby sister named Layla. Layla was by far the cutest thing Jillian had ever seen, and she couldn't wait for Layla and her mommy to come home from the hospital. Jillian and her father had spent pretty much the entire day in her mommy's room but had finally come home a couple of hours ago to get some rest. Jillian hadn't wanted to leave; however, now that she was in bed and preparing to drop off to sleep, she was sort of glad they had. Plus, she was dying to get back to school tomorrow, so she could tell everyone about the amazing new addition to their family.

Jillian breathed deeply and felt herself becoming drowsier by the second. Which was why when her father knocked on her door and walked in, he sort of startled her.

"Did you say your prayers?" he asked, sitting down next to her and turning on the lamp on her nightstand.

"Yes."

"Did you thank God for your new baby sister?"

"Yes. And I thanked Him for you, too. I thanked Him for Mommy and for taking care of all of us."

"Good. Now, give Daddy a big hug."

Jillian smiled and then raised her body up. Her father held her closely, and she felt safe. So much so that she silently thanked God again for blessing her with such a caring father.

But when he released her, he looked at her strangely. He looked at her in a way she'd never seen anyone look at her be-

fore . . . and it was at that very moment
that her sweet little life changed forever.

CHAPTER 1

Five Years Later

After finishing his Sunday-morning sermon, Jillian's pastor took a seat in the pulpit, and the choir sang a song she hadn't heard before. It was a nice song, though, and the words made her think about the one thing she thought about every day of her life: If God loved her so much, why hadn't he saved her from her father? Especially since she always tried her best to be a good girl and was. Everyone said so: her mother, her grandparents, her teachers — everyone. So what she was going through didn't make any sense.

It was true that seven years ago, when her father had first come into their lives, she couldn't have been happier. He'd been so wonderful to her, and it had only been a matter of months before her mom and he had fallen in love and gotten married. They'd wasted no time, and Jillian had been thrilled to finally have her own dad, the same as her cousins, friends, and schoolmates. Of course, not everyone had a dad living in the house with them. For one, her best friend, Nikki, didn't, but for the most part everyone else around her did.

She'd been excited because with the exception of a few old photos, she'd never seen her biological father or even spoken to him by phone. To this very day, he'd never tried contacting her, not in all of her twelve years, and she couldn't help wondering why he didn't want her. She also couldn't help thinking about the conversation she and her mother had had only one month ago.

"Mom, can I ask you something?" Jillian had said one day when the two of them were in the car, heading to a burger joint.

"Sure, sweetie, what is it?"

"Do you think I'll ever see my *real* father?"

At first, her mother hadn't said anything, obviously shocked about the question. But finally, she responded.

"I really don't know."

"Do you think it would be okay if I looked for him?"

There had been more silence, and this time her mother's pause had been longer than it was before.

"Is there something wrong, honey?"

"No."

"And what about the father you have now? Isn't he all that you could have ever hoped for?"

Over the last five years, Jillian had mastered the art of acting, and to prove it, she said, "Oh yes, Mom, he's the best daddy in the world, and I've loved him since the very beginning."

"Then why are you asking about your biological father?"

"I don't know. For some reason I've been thinking about him a lot lately."

Her mother had driven into the parking lot of the burger joint, found a spot to park in, turned off the ignition, and then turned slightly toward Jillian.

"Sweetie, I know I've never said much about your father, but now that you're a lot more curious about him, and rightfully so, I think it's time I tell you everything."

"Like what?"

"Well, first of all, he didn't just leave us. No, TC Maxwell left us while I was still carrying you. I was six months pregnant, and all I know is that one morning I got up and went to work but when I came home, he was gone. He never even had the decency to say good-bye, and he took all the bit of money we had to our names. He left me with nothing, and I was devastated."

Jillian was stunned. "Why did he do that? I mean, didn't he even want to see what I looked like?"

"I don't know, honey. I don't know what was going through his head back then, but a few weeks before he left, all he talked about was how he wanted to move back to Chicago. That was where he lived before I met him, and he never really liked living here in Mitchell. Said it was too slow and not at all like the life he'd become accustomed to. For a number of years, I guess he used to sing in a band and perform at various Chicago nightclubs."

"Well, why didn't you want to go with him?"

"Because he wasn't the most stable person when it came to keeping a job. We only dated for six months and during that time, he quit two different jobs. Then, once we were married, he quit another two jobs during that six-month period. And it was right after that that he walked out."

"And you've never once heard from him since then?"

"No. He called your grandparents a couple of times right before you turned one, but when Mom told him that he needed to come see you, he kept telling her that he was down on his luck and didn't have anything to give you. Mom then told him that you were being well taken care of and that he shouldn't worry about that. She told him that he should come so you could know who your father was."

Jillian had looked away, tears filling her eyes.

"I know it's not the easiest thing to hear, but I really feel like it's time you knew the whole story. And if it wasn't for Mom and Dad, I'm not sure what would have happened to you or me, because the very next week after your father left, they came to help me pack up all my things and then moved me in with them. I'll never forget Mom and how she told me everything was going to be all right and that she and Dad were going to be there for you and me for as long as we needed them to be. They even picked you and me up from the hospital when you were born, and that's why they've always treated you more like a daughter than a grand-daughter."

"I know, and I love them like parents, too. But I still don't understand why my real father hasn't tried to find me — why he doesn't want to see me."

"I don't understand it either, but what I do know is that you are the best thing that came from my marriage to him. You immediately became my greatest joy, and that's why I went to work in a factory only seventeen days after you were born, making sure you didn't go without the things every child needs. We didn't have a lot but with Mom babysitting you, I was able to go to work and pay her for taking care of you. Actually, you never wanted for anything, because when we were staying with Mom and Dad, I paid them rent, but it wasn't nearly as much as I would have had to pay at my own apartment. Plus, *they* spoiled you pretty good as well."

"Then why didn't we just keep living with them?"

"Because after you turned three and I turned twenty-four a few days later, I decided that Mom and Dad deserved to have their house to themselves. They'd been kind enough to take us in, and I will always be thankful for that, but it was time we got our own place. They didn't want to see us go, but I didn't want them feeling as though they were obligated to take care of their grown daughter and a grandchild when it clearly wasn't their responsibility. It made things a lot harder for us financially, but it was definitely the right thing to do."

"I'm sorry my father left you. Especially

since I hadn't even been born yet."

"There's no need for you to apologize at all. None of this was your fault, and if anything, I'm sorry for choosing to marry the kind of man he turned out to be. And that's also the reason I've always been so happy about Byron coming into our lives when he did, because he's such a good man. So much better than my first husband. So kind and so much more compassionate. Byron is truly our gift from God, no doubt about it."

When the congregation applauded, Jillian left her daydream and looked at her mom. The choir had finished singing and now the announcement clerk was strolling toward one of the side podiums. Jillian was sort of getting restless and couldn't wait for service to be dismissed. Not to mention she couldn't wait to get home to her new cherrywood bedroom set. She'd just gotten it last week, thanks to her father, who had said he wanted them to have all new furniture in the new home they'd just purchased and moved into a few months ago — a home her mother had said they never would have been able to afford had it not been for her father. Which was true, and Jillian was definitely thankful to him for all he did, but the only thing was, she didn't know why he had to keep touching her between her legs.

She didn't know why he wouldn't simply keep his hands to himself or find someone else to have his "special times" with. He'd been touching her for five straight years now, and with the way things were going, she didn't see where he was going to be stopping any time soon. She'd even looked the whole thing up on the Internet, right after she'd started her sex education class one year ago, and learned that what he was doing to her had a name. Fondling. That's what the website she'd gone to had called it. She'd also found some other information regarding childhood sexual abuse, but she still wasn't sure she was being "abused," because mostly what she read online were articles about young girls who had been raped. She remembered how she hadn't even known what rape really was, but then she'd looked up the definition of that word, too, and had quickly realized her father hadn't done anything like that to her. Mainly, all he did was caress her private area, or as he called it, her "kitty," and he would kiss her. Although, as of two years ago, he'd changed the *way* he'd been kissing her, because now he always stuck his tongue inside her mouth in a wild and gross sort of way and then made her rub his thing until it became hard. She'd never seen it, but he still made her rub it through whatever pants he was wearing.

It was interesting, though, how he only made her do these horrid things when her mother wasn't home. Jillian wanted so badly to tell her, but her father always reminded her that her mother would blame her for everything and would kick her out of the house for good. He'd also insisted that if she told her grandparents, her little friends, or anyone else, none of those people would understand and they probably wouldn't have anything else to do with her. So it hadn't been long before she'd completely given up on the idea of confiding her secret and had decided this wouldn't last forever. She decided that in six years, she'd be off to college and wouldn't have to worry about any of this again. Plus, she kept telling herself that it was only "fondling" and that maybe it wasn't all that bad.

Jillian snapped back to the present moment when she heard her father's voice. He was speaking before the congregation and had everyone's undivided attention. They'd only been members of True Vine Christian Center for about a year now, but her father had already been appointed a deacon. Partly because he'd known the senior pastor for a number of years, and partly because he'd been ordained as a deacon at the last church they'd joined — which had actually been the second church they'd been members of since her mother and father had gotten married seven years ago, and True Vine was the third. Jillian wasn't sure why they had to keep changing churches; all she knew was that her father would suddenly become tired of "the same old, same old" and out of nowhere, they would move on.

Now he was filling in the congregation on the conversation he'd had earlier in the week with the Sunday school superintendent, regarding the noticeable lack of attendance — something Jillian was shocked about, because with the exception of when he was home or around people he'd known for years, he didn't talk a whole lot. He was pretty much the quiet type and the kind of person who had a hard time making direct eye contact with anyone for longer than a few seconds. Actually, the more Jillian thought about it, there was a slight sneakiness about him, too.

But maybe since he knew this group of people, he was completely comfortable when it came to speaking to them.

"I know some of us tend to slack off a bit when it gets hot outside and that there are so many other summer activities going on. But I just want to encourage you to work a little harder at getting here for Sunday school and here for Wednesday-night Bible study. It'll continue to be pretty warm for at least another month or so, but I still hope you'll start coming back to both sessions a lot more regularly."

Some of the members said, "Amen."

"It is so important for us adults to attend our classes, and it is extremely crucial for us to bring our children as well. To tell you the truth, I'm not sure where I'd be or what kind of terrible person I would have become had my grandparents not brought me to Sunday school every single Sunday morning. Sunday school helped teach me right from wrong, and I know for sure that studying the Bible and learning hundreds and hundreds of life-altering scriptures is the reason I am a true man of God. It is the reason my moral values and family values are so exceptionally strong and why I am able to be a good husband to my wife, Roxanne, and a good father to our daughters."

Jillian wanted to scream. She wanted to stand on her feet and yell out loud what a lying hypocrite her father really was. She wanted to tell all of them that the man they praised and loved wasn't who they thought he was. She wanted desperately to tell them that he was nothing like the wonderful Christian he successfully pretended to be.

But instead, she looked at her mother, who was smiling brightly and looking prouder than the parent of an Olympic gold medalist, and said nothing.

Jillian did smile back at her, though, feigning her adoration and agreement, and then looked back at her father.

"So, church, all I'm asking is that we please take Sunday school and Bible study a little more serious than we have been. Do what you know God wants you to do. For yourselves and also for our children. Thank you."

The congregation applauded again, and her father took his seat on one of the front pews.

Jillian applauded, too, and acted as though life with her loving father just couldn't be better.

Chapter 2

"Service was just wonderful today," Jillian's mom exclaimed to her husband, who stopped his pearl-white SUV at a red light. They were on their way home, and Jillian and Layla were sitting in the backseat.

"Yes, it really was. Pastor gave an amazing sermon."

"I was also very proud of you for making that appeal to the congregation about Sunday school and Bible study. Both are so important, and it was very good of you to share what Sunday school did for you when you were a child."

"It really did make a great difference in my life. It has helped me in so many ways, and because I've always tried to live by God's word, do the right thing, and treat people the way I want to be treated, I truly believe this is why I've been so blessed. Especially blessed to have found someone like you. Someone who loves me so unconditionally and someone I can love back the same way."

"We are definitely a very blessed couple."

Jillian's father glanced at her through his rearview mirror. "And we have two of the sweetest daughters in the world."

Jillian couldn't believe how fooled he had her mother and quickly looked away and out the window. She then looked over at Layla, who had dropped off to sleep. Jillian adored and admired her little sister and suddenly wished she was five again herself, because if she was, she wouldn't have to do the awful things her father so regularly forced her to do.

After about another ten minutes, they pulled into the driveway, waited for the garage to open, and then drove inside. When they got out, they walked into the kitchen, and Jillian's mom said, "Boy, am I glad I prepared our dinner yesterday, because once I change into my sweat suit, all I'll have to do is come back down and warm everything up."

Jillian's father removed his shoes and went into the family room. "I'll change my clothes after dinner because right now, I'm going to see what the Bears are up to."

"Sounds good," her mother said. "Come on, Layla. Let's get you into some play clothes."

Jillian followed her mother and sister up the staircase, walked into her room, and closed the door behind her. She immediately slipped off her fuchsia-colored dress, hung it up in her closet, stepped out of her jet-black pantyhose, and then put on a yellow-and-white Mitchell Junior High T-shirt, along with a pair of matching shorts.

Next, she flipped on her television and called her friend, Nikki.

"Hey, Jill."

"Hey."

"Did you guys just get home from church?"

"Yep. What about you and your mom?"

"We just got home, too, and, girl, I so wish you had come and visited with us today."

"Really?" Jillian said, preparing for whatever juicy gossip Nikki was about to share with her.

"Girl, yeah. You've seen Sister Hanson before."

"Too many times."

"Well, she showed her natural behind this morning. Girl, she shouted so hard and for so long that her wig flew right off of her head!"

Both girls cracked up laughing.

"Get out of here!" Jillian said when she

caught her breath. "Oh my goodness."

"And you know me. I laughed right in the middle of service."

"I know your mom was mad about that, though, wasn't she?"

"Of course. She gave me a dirty look, but I couldn't help myself. That scene was too, too funny."

"I'll bet it was."

"She's such a fake."

"How do you know?"

"Because my mom said so. I overheard her saying that Sister Hanson keeps company with at least four different men and is sleeping with every one of them."

"All at the same time?"

"No, silly. I guess she spends time with each of them on different days."

"Oh. But that's still pretty disgusting."

"I know. And I think it's a shame how she does all that worshipping and shouting at church and then acts like some common whore when she gets home."

Jillian audibly drew in her breath. "Nikki! I can't believe you said that."

"What?"

" 'Whore.' "

"Well, it's not like it's a bad word, because 'whore' is in the Bible."

"Still, though, it's not a very nice word."

"Maybe not, but I'm just repeating what I heard my mom saying about her."

"True."

"So, girl, enough about Sister Hanson. What are you planning to wear to school tomorrow?"

"I don't know. But I was sort of thinking about one of the new jean outfits I haven't worn yet. You know, the dark purple one I showed you last week that my mom bought me right before school started."

"I'll probably wear a jean outfit, too, then, but it won't be a new one. My crazy father has been slacking on my mom's child support payments again, so my mom hasn't been able to get me any more than the five outfits she got me a few weeks ago. And I wore those during the first five days of school last week."

"I got ten, but if you want me to, I'll just wear something old tomorrow, too."

"Girl, no way, because if I had something else new to wear, I would definitely be sporting it. My mom is going to be getting me some more clothes this weekend once she gets paid, though, so I'll be fine."

"That's good."

"I'm just so excited to be in the seventh grade. It was one thing to be in sixth and to finally be out of that baby elementary school, but this is even better. It's so much fun."

"It really is."

"And the boys are so cute and so mature. Especially Marcus."

"You're really liking him, aren't you?"

"Are you kidding? Girl, who doesn't? He's our star quarterback, he's fine, and he's in the eighth grade. Shoot, next year, he'll already be in high school."

"Well, don't forget what I told you I heard."

"What?" Jillian could practically see the frown on her best friend's face right through the phone line.

"You know. That he's been having sex for a whole year now and that he doesn't deal with girls who aren't willing to do that with him."

"Well, it's not like I'm some little girl anyway. In six months, I'll be thirteen and practically a grown woman. Plus, there are a lot of girls at our school who've already done it more than once, so I can't wait to find out what it's like for myself."

"But we're too young to be having sex with boys. You're supposed to wait until you're married before you even think about having sex. Not to mention, having sex before marriage is a sin."

Nikki laughed like she couldn't believe what she'd just heard. "Jill, girl, nobody waits for all of that anymore. And if you don't stop thinking that way, you'll never be able to get or keep a boyfriend."

Jillian thought about her father and all the things he'd been making her do with him. "I don't want one."

"You're just saying that, but when the right boy comes along, you'll change your mind in what my uncle calls a New York minute."

"No, I won't. Because all I want is to get through junior high and high school, and then I can't wait for the day when I can finally head off to college."

"Why are you always saying that? You've been saying that ever since we were seven years old and in the second grade."

"I keep saying it because I want to be a news anchor on CNN, and I can't do that until I finish college. I won't be able to start my career until I graduate from a really good journalism school."

"Pleeease. That's six years away, so I'm not thinking about anything like that. Right now, I'm going to have as much fun as I can, because once we do leave for college, we'll have to spend all of our time studying. Well, actually, you spend all your time doing that now, but still, it'll be even more so once we get to some university."

"Maybe. But that's what I want."

"My mom is always saying that we should enjoy our childhood years as much as we can because life is so much different when you become an adult. Life is so much harder and you have so much responsibility."

Jillian heard what her best friend was saying and for a quick second, she wanted to tell her the real reason she couldn't wait to leave home. But she couldn't. It was true that she really did want to be on CNN one day, delivering the news across national airways, but her primary reason for wanting to leave was her father. She wanted to leave so he'd never be able to touch her again in all the wrong places. If she left, she would never have to touch him again either.

Jillian heard a knock at her door. "Hey, Nik, I'll ring you back after dinner, okay?"

"Okay. See ya."

Jillian hung up the phone. "Come in."

She thought maybe it was her mom, but when she looked up, her father walked in and shut the door. Jillian wondered what he wanted, because in all the years that she'd known him, he'd never come into her room and closed the door while her mother was home.

Her stomach churned as he folded his arms and strutted closer to where she was sitting.

"You sure did look pretty at church today, princess. And for a minute, I almost forgot that you were only twelve years old. You looked more like a twenty-year-old woman."

Jillian never moved an inch and barely blinked her eyes.

Thank God all he did next was smile, walk back toward the door, and open it. "Your mom has dinner on the table, so she wanted me to let you know it was time for you to come down."

"Oh. Thanks."

"You're welcome. See you in a few minutes."

When he left, Jillian breathed a sigh of relief. She'd been so afraid he was going to try something right then and there that she'd almost peed on herself. He made her so nervous whenever he looked at her in the eerie way he had only minutes ago, but now she had to pull herself together. She needed to calm down and put on a genuinely happy face for her mother. She had to make sure her mother didn't suspect even the slightest little thing, because if she did, she knew her mother would blame her for everything and would kick her out on the street like an enemy. She'd get rid of her fast and in a hurry. Just like her father had promised.

CHAPTER 3

The cafeteria at Mitchell Junior High was as noisy as ever, but this was always the most enjoyable part of each school day. Especially since this was the one time Jillian could hang out with all four of her closest friends. Nikki was her BFF, but Ashley and Shelly came in as close seconds.

"I love it when we have lasagna," Ashley announced right after placing a forkful in her mouth. Jillian wasn't surprised, because of the four of them, Ashley clearly had the heartiest appetite and it showed.

"Me, too," Shelly added. "It's one of the best things they make here, but it's so ridiculously full of carbohydrates."

Jillian wasn't shocked by Shelly's comment either, because Shelly spent a noticeable amount of time counting carbs, fat grams, and calories. She was terrified of being overweight and made sure she never ate too much of anything or went more than a day without working out.

Food, however, was the very least of Nikki's worries. "Check it out," she said, looking over at Marcus and three of his teammates, smiling and pointing in their direction. "If they keep it up, I'm gonna take my behind right over there to ask Marcus what he's staring at."

Ashley and Shelly giggled, obviously wanting to flirt with Marcus and his little friends just as much as Nikki did.

Jillian felt just the opposite. "Girl, if you know what's good for you, you'll forget about that boy."

"Why?"

"Remember what I told you on the phone yesterday?"

Nikki waved Jillian off. "Please. I'm not afraid of Marcus or whatever it is he's interested in doing."

Jillian shook her head and before she could say anything else, Nikki was out of her seat and sashaying across the room. Jillian saw the way he smiled at Nikki, along with the creepy way he scanned her body from head to toe, and the look on his face reminded Jillian of her father. She so wished Nikki would stop trying to be so grown all the time and would listen to what she kept trying to tell her. She wished Nikki would leave Marcus alone before she did something she would soon end up regretting.

Ashley drank some grape juice. "Nik is flirting with Marcus big time."

Shelly leaned back in her seat. "I love it. Go, Nikki."

Jillian sighed deeply and then saw Nikki pointing at the three of them and walking back to the table with all four guys. Jillian wasn't happy about this at all, because the last thing she wanted was to have to deal with some boy trying to talk to her.

Nikki introduced them right away. "These are my girls. Jillian, Ashley, and Shelly. Girls, this is Marcus, Darren, Kyle, and Jason."

They all greeted one another, and Jillian couldn't deny that Kyle was just as handsome as Marcus. She also had to admit that he was definitely attracted to her, because while he'd said hello to both Ashley and Shelly, too, he was still smiling at her. Surprisingly, she'd smiled back at him, but then quickly averted her eyes, almost feeling embarrassed.

"Why don't you guys have a seat," Nikki offered.

"Sounds good to me," Marcus responded, and sat next to her.

Kyle, on the other hand, took a chair right

next to Jillian, and her stomach fluttered. "So, are you enjoying the new school year?"

Jillian looked straight ahead. "Yes. You?"

"Yeah, it's cool. Especially since football season has started."

Jillian glanced at him for a second and smiled.

"So, where do you live?" he asked.

"On Taylor Avenue."

"Really? Then I'm only a few blocks away from you, because I live over on Reagan."

"Oh. Yeah, that is close."

"Too bad we don't ride the same bus, hunh?"

She glanced at him again and then looked across the room.

"Why do you keep doing that?"

With reluctance, she turned back toward him but hunched her shoulders.

"It's not like I'm going to bite. You do know that, don't you?"

"Of course I know that."

"Good. Then can I have your phone number?"

She hoped God would forgive her for the lie she was about to tell. "Actually, we just got it changed, and I haven't memorized it yet."

Nikki, through all of her conversation with Marcus and the rest of them, heard Jillian's answer and gazed at her with a confused demeanor. But Jillian ignored her.

Kyle still wasn't giving up, though. "Can I get it from you tomorrow, then?"

"Yeah, if I remember it."

They all chatted about the upcoming game and the school dance that would be happening in a couple of weeks, and then the guys stood up. Jillian saw Nikki passing a slip of paper to Marcus, with what she was sure was Nikki's phone number, and then the boys said their good-byes.

"Oh my God," Nikki began. "Marcus is so outrageously fine, and I could tell from the moment I walked over to them that he wants me bad."

"He definitely does, girl," Shelly agreed.

"And what about Kyle?" Ashley said. "Darren and Jason look okay, but they're not nearly as fine as Kyle. And Jill, girl, he was practically drooling all over you."

Shelly gave Ashley a high five, and said, "I know that's right."

Jillian downplayed their observation. "Whatever."

"You know it's true," Nikki chimed in. "Which is the reason I wanna know why you lied when he asked you for your phone number."

"I'm not thinking about that boy."

Nikki laughed. "Well, you sure don't sound very convincing. And I don't understand what the big deal is anyway because as you can see, I gave Marcus *my* phone number and e-mail address faster than he could ask for it."

The other two girls seemed to be just as excited as Nikki, and there was a part of Jillian that wished she could feel the same way. But she couldn't. Not with all the madness she'd been experiencing with her father. She knew it wasn't normal for a twelve-year-old girl to *not* be overly excited about some cute little boy who was interested in her, but truth be told, she really didn't know how she should feel about boys or how she should act when they approached her. She did like Kyle but at the same time, she knew if she started talking to him, there was a chance he might try to pressure her into doing certain things — the kind of things she and her father engaged in at home on a regular basis — and she would never be able to handle that. So, to her, it was just best to keep her distance from Kyle and any other boy at her school. It was best to keep to herself as much as possible before someone peeped out her secret. The deep, dark, and very dirty secret

she and her father had been keeping for
years.

CHAPTER 4

Jillian grabbed her brown nylon book bag and brown leather shoulder purse off the car seat. "Thanks for the ride, Miss G."

"No problem, sweetie. See you tomorrow."

"I'll call you later, Nik."

"Okay, talk to you then."

Jillian stepped out of the vehicle and then waved good-bye to her best friend and her best friend's mom, Miss Gordon. But as they pulled away and she turned and saw her father's SUV inside the garage, her heart plummeted. She wasn't sure where her mother was because normally she was home from work whenever Jillian arrived later than usual. Her father was sometimes already home by five o'clock as well, with him working what he called flex hours, and this was also the reason Jillian had made sure to sign up for one of the key clubs and yearbook staff, and why she occasionally volunteered at a nearby nursing home. This way, she was guaranteed not to make it home before her mother on at least two days per week and would have much less of a chance of being home alone with her father. But today, for some reason, her mother wasn't there yet, and now she wished she'd asked Miss G if she could go home with them for a while. Miss G got off work around four, so she'd told Jillian's mom that on the days the girls had extracurricular activities, she had no problem at all with picking them up. Jillian's mom had been very thankful for this and in return, she helped out with the cost of Miss G's gas each week. Actually, Jillian was somewhat shocked that Nikki had even considered joining either of the groups she was involved in, but it hadn't been long before Jillian realized it was all because Nikki had seen a couple of cute boys in each of them. Then, as far as the nursing home went, Jillian was sure that the only reason Nikki had wanted to volunteer there was because her grandmother was one of the residents.

Jillian walked inside the house, looked around, but didn't see or hear her father. Maybe he was out with her mom. That's what she was hoping for, anyway, and she was kind of relieved — relieved enough to kick off her shoes, grab a couple of chocolate chip cookies from the large glass jar on the kitchen counter, and then pour herself a cup of milk. She sat for a few minutes until she finished eating and drinking and then went upstairs to her room. Once there, she performed her normal ritual: dropped her bags on top of her desk, turned on the television, laid across the bed on her stomach, and flipped through the channels until she saw *That's So Raven.*

She watched for a couple of minutes and was already laughing at something Raven had just said. She loved this show, new episodes or reruns, and she rarely missed it.

But just as a commercial came on, Jillian flinched in fear. She saw her door opening and to her regret, it was her father. He must have been in his and her mom's bedroom and had purposely kept quiet, so he could catch her off guard.

Jillian quickly sat up and backed closer to her pillows and headboard.

"So, how was your day, princess?"

"Fine. Where's Mom?"

"She dropped Layla off at your grandparents' and then went to dinner with some of the ladies she works with. She'll be gone at least another couple of hours."

Jillian's heart beat faster than normal, and

she wished her father would just leave. Leave her room and leave her alone. But he didn't. Instead, he did his usual. Sat down on the side of her bed.

"I'm so proud of you, princess. You know that?"

Jillian stared at him but didn't respond.

"I'm proud because I know you're going to do so well in school again this year. You're such an intelligent young lady, and you're so caring. Which is why you're the most precious thing in my life. I mean, don't get me wrong, Layla is my actual blood daughter and I love her with all my heart, but you're the one who's the most important to me."

Jillian still didn't say anything, but then her father smiled and stroked the side of her face. Then he stood up. Which was strange because normally when they had their time together, he always sat or lay next to her on her bed. Never under the covers, but always very close to her.

"Princess, Daddy needs you to do something different for him today, okay?"

Jillian tried forcing down the lump in her throat. "What?"

"It's something very important to me. Something that will make Daddy feel better than his little princess has ever made him feel."

She had no idea what he was talking about, but she still had a really bad feeling about all of this. Not because he'd just closed her shades and turned off the television, because he did this all the time, but because for the first time ever, she heard him unbuckling his belt and unzipping his pants.

"Come closer to the edge of the bed."

He was still standing, so none of this made much sense to her until she thought back to what she'd read on the Internet and then she thought about the time this boy had asked Nikki to . . .

"Sweetheart, Daddy needs you to open your mouth real wide, okay? As wide as you can."

"Daddy, no. Please don't make me do this."

"This won't take long at all, princess. I promise."

"Daddy, please. I'm begging you, please don't make me."

"Jillian, are you being disobedient again? Because you know God doesn't like it when young girls don't do what their parents tell them."

"But, Daddy —"

"Look, Jillian. You know I don't like it when you whine like this, so stop it."

He was calling her by her first name and his voice was stern, so she knew he meant business.

"Now, open your mouth," he said, taking the side of her face and pulling her closer to him.

Tears flooded her cheeks. "Daddy, I can't."

"You can and you will. Now, do you want your mom to find out that you've been disobeying me? Do you want me to pack my things and leave?"

"No."

"Then do as I tell you."

Jillian pressed her lips together as tightly as she could, but then finally gave up on trying to resist him. She opened her mouth, and he forced himself inside of it. She gagged immediately and could barely breathe. But her father paid no attention and instead instructed her on what exactly she needed to do.

"Come on, princess, all you have to do is suck it the same exact way you suck a lollipop. It's that easy."

Jillian was clueless and tried pulling away from him, but he was holding her head very steady and she couldn't move.

"I won't keep repeating myself. Now, do what I told you."

Jillian wept and then did the best she could. This was the most awful thing she'd ever done. Her father, however, made lots of weird noises and seemed as though he had traveled to a different galaxy. He moaned and groaned like a person in great pain, but at the same time he seemed to be enjoying himself completely.

This, of course, was the total opposite of what Jillian was feeling, because at this very moment, she wanted to die. She wished she'd never been born or, better yet, that her mother had never married her father in the first place. She wished her mother had never met him, period.

She couldn't wait for this to be over with, and for the first time, she prayed for something very bad to happen to her father. Anything at all, as long as she never had to see him again.

CHAPTER 5

Jillian lay in her bed, balled up like a newborn baby. She'd been lying there for at least two hours, but no matter how hard she tried, she couldn't stop thinking about what had just happened to her. Her father had actually made her give him oral sex, and now she was trying with all her might to figure out if this kind of sex was considered just as real as sexual intercourse.

Over the last year, she'd been Googling and checking other online search engines for as much information as she could find, trying to educate herself on a number of items, but she was still a bit confused about whether oral sex fell into a different category. Some people said it did, some said it didn't. Some said you were still an innocent virgin if all you'd done was give oral sex to someone and some said you weren't. Either way, though, the one thing she did know was that what she'd done with her father, not long ago, was as wrong as wrong could be.

Jillian thought about the way he'd forced himself down her throat and cried all over again. This was an absolute nightmare, and no matter what she did, she just couldn't seem to wake up from it. It just wouldn't go away.

Maybe her father was crazy. Maybe he had some mental problem that her mother hadn't known about when she'd met him. Because surely no normal person would do the things he was doing with her — things he'd been doing since she was seven years old. Surely, a grown man like him would much rather do these things with an adult woman. Surely, he would only want to do them with her mother.

Then, the whole idea that when he'd left her room, he hadn't even bothered zipping his pants back up seemed noticeably insane as well. Yes, no one else was home, but it still didn't seem right, and it was almost like he didn't care. Not to mention, on his way out, he'd told her to go into the bathroom to wash her face with cold water, because the last thing her mother needed to see was that she'd been crying about nothing.

Jillian had, of course, followed his instructions but had wiped tears the entire time. When she'd finished in the bathroom, she'd climbed back into bed and thankfully hadn't heard anything else from him. Although, now, she heard the doorbell ringing and wondered who it could be.

She lay quietly for a few minutes, but then she heard her father calling out to her, so she opened her bedroom door. "Yes."

"Princess, your grandparents just brought Layla home, and they want to see you."

At first, Jillian paused. Then she said, "Okay."

Normally, Jillian was thrilled to see her grandparents, but not today. Not when she was feeling stunned, out of sorts, and just plain distraught. She was still in shock and had spent much of the last hour trying to remember what she'd done to deserve such gruesome treatment. Her mother had raised her to love, honor, and trust God with everything in her, but her love, honor, and trust were beginning to fade, because for the life of her, she couldn't understand why God was allowing this dreadful thing to happen between her and her father. Maybe God was punishing her because of how when she was five she'd taken a long stick and poked their parrot, over and over, every single day, as soon as she arrived home from school, and always when her mother wasn't in the room with them. For some strange reason, she'd gotten a huge kick out of taunting the colorful little creature, but now maybe it was payback time and this was God's way of doing it.

I didn't mean it, God. I'm so sorry for doing that, and I'm also sorry for the time when I was four and Mom asked me if I'd broken her vase and I told her that the little girl down the street had done it and ran home. I'm so, so sorry.

Jillian straightened out her clothing, removed her scrunchie, brushed her hair into a fresh ponytail, and went downstairs.

"Hi, sweetheart," her grandma, Naomi, said, hugging her.

"Hi, Grandma. Hi, Grandpa," she said, now hugging her grandfather.

"Hi, Grandbaby. How are you?"

"I'm fine."

Now that she was standing directly in front of them, she actually was happy to see her grandparents and hadn't felt this safe in a long time. She wished she could stay in her grandfather's arms forever or, even better, go home to live with them for good. If only she had the courage to tell them everything, so that she would never have to come back here. But her father had made it clear that her grandparents would be just as furious as her mother and would never have anything else to do with her. He'd made it clear that if their special secret ever got out, their entire family would be ruined and it would be all her fault. He insisted that everyone would hate her from then on.

"Look, Jill," Layla said, rushing toward her big sister with a drawing. "Look what I made in school today."

"How pretty, Layla. You're so talented, and the colors are so beautiful."

"Thank you, Jill."

"You're welcome."

"I made it for you."

"Really?"

"Yep. So, are you going to put it on your wall in your room?"

"Sure. We'll put it up tonight."

"Yayyyyy," Layla said, and ran up the staircase to watch either Disney or Nickelodeon, Jillian was sure.

Their father got up from the sofa. "Carter and Naomi, if you don't mind, I'm going to run to the office supply store."

"Son, go right ahead," Carter said.

"That's right," Naomi added.

"Do the two of you need anything while I'm out?"

"No, honey," Naomi said. "We're fine."

"Sounds good," he said, and then looked at Jillian. "Can I get you anything, princess?"

Jillian was really starting to despise this word "princess," and she wished he would stop calling her that. "No, thank you."

"Okay, then, I'll see you all when I get back."

I hope not, was all Jillian could think, and she wished she had the nerve to say it straight to his face.

Her grandmother smiled. "So, how was school today?"

"It was good."

"Are you already getting a lot of homework?"

"Not really. Well, actually, we sort of are this week. But not last week."

"I can't believe my grandbaby is already in seventh grade," her grandfather said. "And whether you realize it or not, these are the best years of your life. Junior high, high school, and then college."

"I know, and I'm already having a lot of fun," she said, trying to sound as bubbly as possible when what she wanted to do was sob like a baby. But she could never let on or cause them to suspect that anything was wrong.

"You haven't spent the night with us in a

while, so maybe you can do it this weekend."

"That would be great, Grandma. And can Nikki stay, too?"

"Of course."

"I'll make sure she asks her mom tonight if it's okay."

Jillian had turned toward the kitchen when she heard someone coming from the garage and saw that it was her mother.

Her mother walked into the family room, hugged Jillian, and sat down next to her. "Mom and Dad, thanks so much for watching Layla and for bringing her home. Especially since Byron had to work a lot later today."

Jillian looked at her mom and wondered why she thought her father had worked late when, in reality, he had arrived home at his normal time and maybe even earlier. But she knew why. She knew he'd purposely told her mother that lie because he'd wanted extra time alone with her. He was so slick and so sneaky, and he got away with anything he wanted without a single question from anyone.

"So, how was your day, sweetie?" her mother asked.

"Fine."

"Are you okay?"

"Yes. Why?"

"Because you seemed like you were in deep thought about something."

"I was just thinking about some homework that I need to get done."

"Are you sure you weren't maybe daydreaming about some new little boy at school?"

Her mom and grandparents laughed, and Jillian, using her sophisticated Academy Award–winning skills, laughed right along with them. "No, Mom, that's not it at all."

"Okay, whatever you say, but remember, I was once twelve going on thirteen myself. Not that you're old enough to be dating boys, because you're certainly not, but still."

Jillian thought about Kyle and how cute he was and then blushed.

"See, that's what I thought," her mother said.

Her grandparents teased her as well, and for a while, she felt happy and was enjoying this great time she was having with the people who loved her.

But then her father came back home and soon took a seat with the rest of them.

"So, how's the job going?" Grandpa Carter asked him.

"Couldn't be better, and as a matter of fact, I just learned last week that I might be up for another promotion. You know I was just promoted to claims supervisor two years ago, but now they're talking group manager."

Jillian's mother beamed with pride. "Isn't that such wonderful news, Mom and Dad?"

"It sure is," Naomi said.

"We're really proud of you, son," Carter told him.

"Thank you."

"And your parents must be just as proud as well."

"They are, and when I called them this afternoon, they were both saying how they wish they lived a lot closer. I mean, it's not like they live in California, but Atlanta is still pretty far away from here."

"I know it must be hard," Naomi said.

Jillian's mother beamed with pride — again. "We're all very proud of you, baby, and no one deserves it more than you do."

Jillian looked on in silence, until her mom said, "Isn't that right, Jill? Doesn't your daddy deserve the best job they have to offer? He deserves the best of everything."

"Yep," she said, smiling, and then wondered if her mother would still feel the same way if she knew what "Daddy" was doing behind his wife's back. She wondered what all of them would say, her grandparents, her father's coworkers, everyone in the neighborhood, and all of their church members. She even wondered how many other young girls were being molested by their fathers, their fathers' fathers, their uncles, brothers, or cousins, in shameful secrecy. Hundreds, thousands, or was it maybe even millions?

Most of all, she wondered why she couldn't bring herself to tell anyone about her own situation. She wanted to tell at least someone, but she knew she'd be in deep trouble. She knew she'd end up in some scary foster home and would probably never see her family again. She knew everyone would disown her and that she'd be worse off than she was already.

She knew she was trapped with no possible way out and that there wasn't a single thing she could do about it.

CHAPTER 6

Today was another day, but Jillian still couldn't shake what had happened less than twenty-four hours ago with her father. It was all so unfair, and she was so distressed over it. She'd even, for the first time in years, considered missing school because she hadn't wanted to face anyone. What she'd wanted was to lock herself in her room, climb back into bed, and hide from the rest of the world. Which had been an okay idea until she thought about her father and how if he found out about it, he might just slip home from work. Needless to say, taking a chance on that was out of the question.

"What I'd like for all of you to do tonight is spend some time writing about something you feel very strongly about," Mrs. Peterson, Jillian's English teacher, said. "You can write anything you want as long as it's written with genuine feeling, and I want it to be at least two pages. Then, over the next two days, I'll have everyone read what they've written out loud to the entire class."

Jillian loved writing and couldn't wait to get started. She wasn't sure what topic she'd choose to focus on, but she knew it would be either the dangers of smoking or parents who abuse their children. She was thinking more about the latter because no matter how many years had passed, she never forgot about the little boy who had lived next door to her and her mom and how his father would get sloppy drunk and then beat the daylights out of him and his mother. Jillian had been only six, but she remembered all of it, and it always saddened her when she heard about any child being physically abused. There were times when she even had to admit that while her own situation with her father was unbearable, at least he never left her with any scars or bruises. At least she was a lot better off than little Bradley had been, and she should probably just be thankful for that.

"What if the subject we want to write about isn't something we want to read in front of the whole class?" one girl wanted to know.

"Then you might want to choose something different, because for this particular

60

assignment, I want you to work on your writing and also your presentation skills. When you get up in front of the class, it won't be the same as if you were giving a formal speech, but I still want you to get used to the idea of sharing your thoughts and feelings with a medium-size group of people."

Dawson, the class clown, a boy Jillian had shared sixth-grade English with last year, raised his hand next.

"Yes, Dawson."

"Mrs. Peterson, can we write a lot more than two pages?"

"Of course. Is that what you're planning to do?"

"No, not me. But last year whenever our teacher would tell us to write a couple of pages, Jillian would always turn in at least a thousand of them. She would write so many pages that we could barely see Mr. Stevens's face once she sat them all down in front of him! Isn't that right, Jillian?"

Just about everyone in the class laughed, and Jillian couldn't help laughing with them. Dawson was clearly exaggerating, but she also couldn't deny that she always wrote a lot more than they were assigned.

Mrs. Peterson looked at Jillian and smiled. "Well, that's actually a good thing. Writing was always my favorite thing to do when I was young, too, so, Miss Jillian, I'll be looking forward to reading every word."

Jillian smiled back at her and for some reason she really liked Mrs. Peterson. She'd liked her from the very first moment she'd met her last Monday, and she'd known right away that she was going to be her favorite teacher this year. She was very pretty, looked as though she was maybe in her late twenties, and there was no doubt that she really loved her job. Jillian had already thought about how she couldn't wait to get started on her paper, but now she couldn't wait to see what Mrs. Peterson would think of it once she finished it.

When the buzzer rang, everyone scattered like ants, leaving the classroom in a hurry. Jillian was almost out the door when Mrs. Peterson stopped her.

"Jillian, do you have a second?"

"Sure, Mrs. Peterson."

"So, you like to write a lot, huh?"

"Well, sort of."

"What kinds of things do you enjoy writing? Poetry? Do you write about your own life in a journal?"

"No. I never, ever write about my own life," Jillian said more loudly than normal, and she could tell that Mrs. Peterson seemed a little taken aback.

Jillian quickly tried cleaning up her tone and hoped Mrs. Peterson hadn't suspected anything. "Sometimes I do write poetry, though, but mostly what I write are short stories."

"Really?"

"Yes."

"How many do you think you've written?"

"I don't know. Maybe ten or so."

"That's wonderful. Would you like me to read them sometime?"

"That would be okay, but I haven't written anything in a few months, so first, I'd like to reread them and make them the best that they can be before I show them to you."

"That sounds fair. Is there some reason you haven't been writing lately?"

Jillian knew exactly why, but she would never own up to it. She knew full well that it was all because of what her father was doing to her. It was because she had to spend a lot of her free time trying to figure out ways not to be home alone with him and a lot of time pretending that she had the perfect childhood — she had to spend a great deal of time creating her own *real-life* work of fiction.

"I did a lot of stuff this summer, and now I'm in an after-school club and do some volunteering. Plus I do stuff at church with our youth department sometimes."

"That's understandable, but if you like writing, maybe you could start back up by just committing thirty minutes per night."

"Okay."

"I also encourage all writers to write about their day-to-day experiences, because somehow I just think it's good for the soul. It's good practice, too, and you don't have to write a lot. Even a paragraph or a page would be fine."

Jillian nodded.

"Do you have a journal?"

"Yes. Last year, my mom bought me this journal and pen set as one of my Christmas gifts, but I've never used it."

"Well, maybe you could pull it out and start adding a few entries."

"Maybe."

"Okay, well, you'd better get to lunch."

"Thanks, Mrs. Peterson."

"You're quite welcome, Jillian."

On the way out of her classroom, she practically bumped right into Kyle.

"Hey, what's up?" he said.

"Hi."

"You said you'd give me your number today, so I figured I'd wait for you here."

"Oh."

"Oh? Well, what does that mean?"

"Nothing, really."

"Are you headed to the cafeteria?"

"Yep, but first I have to meet up with Nikki."

"I'll just walk there with you, then."

Jillian wasn't sure why she felt so nervous, but she'd have been lying if she said she didn't like Kyle. Ever since yesterday, she'd been trying not to, but she could tell she did.

When they arrived at her locker, Nikki was waiting as planned.

"So, are you still going to give me your number?" Kyle asked, and this time Jillian wrote it down on a piece of notebook paper, tore it out, and passed it to him.

"I'll call you this evening, once I get home from practice. See ya."

Nikki nudged Jillian and spoke under her breath. "I knew it. I knew you liked him, girl."

Jillian tried masking her smile. "Whatever."

"Just admit it, you're feeling him just as much as I'm feeling Marcus."

"Are boys all you think about?"

"You'd better believe it, because what else is there?"

"School. Your education. And I can think

of a lot of other things, too."

"Well, right now, Marcus is all I care about. He's so mature and so, so cool. He doesn't talk like the rest of these little boys around here, and he's soooo cute."

Jillian rolled her eyes, but not so that Nikki could see her.

"And I did tell you that he already asked me to be his girl, didn't I?"

"Yeah, you told me," Jillian said as they started toward the lunchroom. "But I just hope you know that once you become his girl, it will only be a matter of time before he wants you to have sex with him."

"And? Because I already told you, I'm ready for anything he wants me to do."

"And I keep telling you that we're too young to be doing that kind of stuff."

"Girl, will you please stop being so serious?" Nikki said, chuckling. "I mean, young people have sex all the time, so it's not like it's some big deal."

Jillian disagreed but knew there was no way she was changing Nikki's mind about this or anything else she was adamant about doing. They were best friends for life, but in some ways, they couldn't have been more different, and it was better to change the subject altogether. "So, how was math class today?"

■ ■ ■ ■

As soon as Jillian got home, she ate dinner with her parents and Layla and then rushed up to her room to write her paper. For the rest of her school day, she'd been thinking about which topic to go with and had decided on the one about abused children. But as she tried drafting the first sentence, she realized she couldn't find the words, something that wasn't very common for her, since she always had a lot to say about everything when it came to writing.

Finally, though, after sitting with her pen and blank sheets of paper, she wrote,

What has been happening to me for the last five years should never happen to any child.

Then, next thing she knew, one sentence quickly turned into another and then another, and before long, she had one full page. Then, without realizing it, she wrote ten more of them. Not once could she remember writing so many words in only one sitting, but it was as if it had all come pouring out of her, and she couldn't stop it. She'd written without even doing much thinking, and it had felt quite natural.

She turned back to the first page, preparing to read the entire thing, but the phone rang. She looked at the Caller ID screen and saw the words "Davis, Kyle."

She quickly picked up the receiver. "Hello?"

"Hey, what's up?"

"Not much. What's up with you?"

"I just finished dinner, and now I'm getting ready to read my science chapters. After that, I have to write my English paper."

"I have an English paper to do, too."

"I figured you did. When I met you outside of your classroom earlier, I forgot to tell you that I have Mrs. Peterson, too. So I guess she's giving both her seventh- and eighth-grade classes the same assignment for tonight."

"Maybe so."

"Mrs. Peterson is one of my favorites."

"I like her, too. A lot."

"So, have you written anything yet?"

"I wrote some stuff just before you called, but that's not what I'm going to turn in."

"Oh."

There was silence after that, but finally Jillian said, "So, is your dad's name Kyle, too?"

"Actually, it is. Why do you ask?"

"Because I saw it on our Caller ID

screen."

"Oh. Yeah, he's Kyle Sr., and I'm Kyle Jr."

"Oh."

Silence again.

Kyle sure didn't sound as cool as he did when they were at school, and Jillian was a little surprised by that. He seemed almost nervous. More nervous than she was.

"So, you know I like you, don't you?" Kyle asked.

"Yeah . . . I guess."

"I liked you from the first day I saw you, even before that day Marcus and all of us came over to your lunch table."

"I like you, too," she said without planning to.

"I could tell right away that you weren't as silly as a lot of the other seventh-grade girls and even some of the eighth-grade ones, and I like that."

Jillian smiled.

"And I can also tell that you're nothing like your girl, Nikki."

"Why do you say that?"

"Because you weren't trying to be all over some guy who only cares about one thing. And it's not like he only wants to do it with just her. Marcus has sex all the time, but he has pretty much no respect at all for girls that come after him the way Nikki is."

69

Jillian didn't like what she was hearing, although she'd tried her best to make Nikki leave that boy alone. "I've already tried talking to her about Marcus."

"And that's basically all you can do. But still, she needs to chill and stop trying to act so grown all the time."

Jillian wanted to agree with him, but she would never bad-mouth her best friend. She would never tell him the truth. That Nikki had been obsessed with boys for as long as she could remember.

"So, are you able to have company?" he asked.

"Yes, but not boys. Sorry."

"Sorry about what?"

"Not being able to have you over."

Kyle laughed.

"What's so funny?"

"Well, I guess because I don't know that many parents around here who will let their twelve-year-old daughters have boys at their house, anyway. I was just asking, but I already assumed what your answer would be."

"Oh."

"We can just hang at school and talk on the phone just like we're doing now."

"And you're okay with that?"

"Yeah. Definitely. But hey, I'd better go so

I can get my homework finished."

"Okay."

"But I'll see you tomorrow, though."

"See ya then. Bye."

Jillian hung up the phone and took a deep breath. She really did like him, and he seemed so much nicer than Marcus. She couldn't wait to see him and talk to him again.

Next, she opened her notebook back up and began reading what she'd written.

What has been happening to me for the last five years should never happen to any child. Not ever. Not in a million lifetimes. Not even to the most terrible child on earth.

Then to think that the first time my father molested me was the very day Layla was born. Daddy and I had come home from the hospital that evening and as soon as I'd changed into my pajamas, he'd come into my room and asked me if I'd said my prayers. Then he told me how special I was and that because he now had two daughters, it was very important for him to prove to me that he would never love me any less than he always had. He showed me by kissing me the way I'd seen him kissing Mom. I remember how I had backed away from him immediately, pulled the covers up to my neck as tightly as I could, and told him I wanted to go to sleep. Still, though, he pulled the covers away from me and insisted that there was nothing wrong with fathers and daughters showing their true love for each other and that fathers and daughters did this all the time. Again, I pulled the covers back up to my neck, but this time he told me how God punishes all children who don't do what their parents tell them and that God always punished them in a very harsh way. He asked me if I wanted God to be angry with me, if I wanted him to tell Mom that I had disobeyed him, or if I wanted him to leave Mom, Layla, and me all alone. Of course, I quickly said no and the next thing I knew, he was reminding me about that commandment in the Bible — the one about honoring thy father and mother — and because I didn't want God to be mad at me, I didn't want to go to hell, and I didn't want Mom to have to take care of Layla and me all by herself, I gave up trying to fight him. I gave up, and Daddy slid his hand inside my pink Dora the Explorer cotton panties and promised me that all he was doing was tickling me.

Then to think how happy I'd been to finally have a father. I was so excited. But now I know that when some adults say be careful what you wish for, they are right. I wished and prayed for a father all the time, but had I known the kind of father I was going to end up with, I would have stopped wishing and praying long before my mom met him. It is interesting how some people can appear to be the nicest, quietest, most caring people on the outside, but behind closed doors they are the most evil people you ever want to meet. They are a child's worst nightmare, and in most cases, no one ever figures them out. No one ever suspects that some nice, quiet men who go to church every single Sunday morning and every Wednesday night and who have good-paying jobs are touching their daughters in places they shouldn't. No one would ever believe that men like my father would even dream of forcing their nasty dingalings down their daughter's throat and then telling her it's no different than placing a piece of candy in her mouth. No one would believe that men like my father would tongue kiss their own daughter in her bedroom and then do the same thing with his wife when she gets home from work an hour later.

Over the next few minutes, Jillian continued reading until she'd read the last word and then fought back loads of tears. She'd been well aware of all that had been happening to her since second grade, but it hadn't been until this evening that it had become so much more of a wretched reality. She was only twelve years old, for God's sake, so what was her father thinking? What was it that had drawn him to her in the first place? What in the world was making him want to do such sinful and shameful things? To a child who was only in seventh grade?

Jillian closed her notebook, the one she would now have to find a good hiding spot for, wiped her face with both hands, and asked God to please deliver her from this craziness. She begged Him to fix whatever was wrong with her father so that from this moment on, he would no longer come into her room when her mother wasn't home, making her do things she didn't want to do. She prayed that from this day forth, she would finally be able to live a happy and very normal life — the kind of life she could be proud of and extremely thankful for.

CHAPTER 7

It was shortly after five a.m., but Jillian was already up, writing another paper for her English class. She'd found a very safe place for the one she'd written last night, so that later this evening she could transfer every word of it into her journal, and now she was writing the new one on the dangers of smoking. She had originally planned to write one on child abuse, but after writing about her own problems, it now seemed much too similar, and she was still very emotional about it. She hadn't thought what her father was doing to her was a form of physical abuse, but now she wasn't so sure.

"Good morning, sweetie," her mom said, knocking and walking into her room.

"Good morning, Mom."

"I thought I heard some moving around in here. What are you doing up so early?"

"Doing homework. I did it last night, but I decided I wanted to turn in something different."

"Oh, okay. Actually, the reason I'm up, too, is because I need to get to work a little earlier so I can have a meeting with my staff."

Jillian's mom was a customer service manager who supervised both lobby and drive-thru tellers, and she also supervised the people who opened new accounts.

"Is Layla up?"

"No, your dad is going to drop her off on his way to work, so he'll be leaving a little early as well."

Jillian was so relieved because this meant he and Layla would be leaving before she did, and she wouldn't have to worry about him bothering her.

"So, how do you like all of your teachers this year?"

"I like them a lot."

"What about little Miss Nikki?"

"She likes all of hers, too, but mostly Nikki is concerned about this boy named Marcus."

Her mother laughed. "Nikki's been liking boys since I can remember, so I'm sure it's just another one of her little crushes."

"Yeah, Mom, but this is different because a lot of kids keep saying that Marcus only likes girls who have sex."

"Well, I'm sure Nikki isn't thinking about doing anything like that. And I certainly hope you're not thinking about anything like that either, are you?"

"No."

"Good, because peer pressure is hard, and I know twelve-year-old girls start becoming pretty curious about things like that. But trust me, Jill, having sex at a very young age just isn't worth it. It's the worst thing you can do, and it's so much better for a young lady to hold on to her innocence for as long as possible. It's better to wait until you meet a nice young man and get married to him. I know as you get older, you'll have a lot of questions and concerns, though, so I want you to know that you can come to me about anything, sweetie. Anything at all. Good or bad. And I want you to always remember that, okay?"

"Yes, Mom," Jillian said, and then wondered if she still had the kind of innocence her mother was talking about. Especially since she still hadn't had actual intercourse. She had so many questions and what she wanted, at this very moment, was to tell her mother everything. She wanted to tell her, but what if her father was right? *Your mother will blame you for everything, and she'll kick you out of the house for good. Our entire fam-*

ily will be ruined, it'll be all your fault, and everyone will hate you from now on.

What if her mother would never speak to her again? What if she really would hate her from then on? But then again, she was her mother, and mothers loved their daughters.

Her mom continued. "And then if you feel like you can't come to me, you always have your grandparents and also your father. Byron loves you as if you were his own, and I think I'm more happy and proud about that than I am about anything else. It's not every day a single mother can find a man who will love her and a child she already has. Byron is such a huge blessing to you and me and your little sister, and I can't even imagine how life would be without him. Actually, at this point in my life, I don't think I *could* live without him."

The verdict was in. Telling her mother about her father was a very bad idea, and all she could do now was keep praying for things to get better. What she had to do was pray harder than ever before that her father would lose interest in their "special times" together. That he would have his "special times" only with his wife.

Her mother walked over to where she was sitting. "Okay?"

"Yes."

Then she kissed Jillian on her forehead. "Now, I'd better get ready, and you have a good day at school. Oh, and I almost forgot to tell you. The bank has me attending a workshop in Chicago next month, so I'll be gone on a Monday, Tuesday, and Wednesday."

"So, you're going to have to drive back and forth all three days?"

"Well, I was going to, but your dad convinced me to go ahead and stay at the hotel with everyone else. I didn't want to leave him with so much responsibility, but he said he was glad to take care of you and Layla by himself and that I deserved a break, anyway. Which I sort of do, sweetie, so I'm kind of looking forward to it."

Jillian felt like she was going to pass out and more than anything, she wanted to get down on her knees and beg her mother not to go.

But she didn't.

"I know you'll miss me, but it'll only be for three days. I'll drive in with everyone else on Monday morning, and then I'll be back on Wednesday evening."

Jillian smiled as authentically as she could, and her mom left the room.

It was one thing for her father to wait until her mother wasn't home, but having her gone for three straight days was another. He'd be able to do whatever he wanted before Layla woke up in the mornings and after she went to sleep in the evenings. This had always been one of Jillian's worst fears, being left alone with him for days at a time, and she was horrified. But like so many other things in her life, there was nothing she could do about it — nothing except what she'd already been doing earlier: praying for the best.

As soon as Jillian heard her father and Layla leaving out of the driveway, she jumped into the shower. She only had an hour before she needed to be at her bus stop, so she really had to get a move on. She could tell it was a little chilly this morning just by the temperature in her bedroom, so the warm water felt good.

She stood there for a minute or so, then lathered her entire body and finally rinsed all the suds away.

"Hey, princess," her father said, coming into the bathroom.

Jillian quickly backed all the way against the far wall, and her father eased open the glass door.

"Don't you look gorgeous this morning, and now I'm so glad I forgot some of my work documents and had to run back inside the house to get them."

Jillian knew he was lying and that he'd only come back in because he wanted to mess with her. Now she could kick herself for not locking the bathroom door, even though she hadn't thought she needed to. "Where's Layla?"

"She's in the car," he said, pulling a digital camera from behind his back. "Wow, princess. You are such a beautiful girl."

Jillian hurried and turned the front of her body away from him. "Daddy, please leave me alone."

But the camera clicked and flashed anyway.

"Turn around so Daddy can take one more picture, and then I'll leave."

"No!"

"Well, if you don't, then I guess I'll have to have Layla come back inside, and then I'll have to miss work, and you'll have to miss school. Which is fine for me because all I have to do is call in sick, but you'll have to explain to your mom why you played hooky today."

Jillian was so ashamed. Even more so today, because strangely enough, he had never seen her completely naked. But she knew he meant what he said and saw no choice except turning around and facing him. She covered her breasts as much as she could, and her father snapped two photos.

"Now. That wasn't bad at all, was it? And what this means is that now Daddy can see his little princess any time he wants, even when I'm at work."

Jillian looked away from him, crying a river of tears. Her father leaned into the shower, kissed her on the cheek, and told her, "I love you, princess."

When he left, Jillian stepped out of the shower, wrapped a bath towel around her body, and gazed into the mirror. She stared into it for a few minutes and then came to a major realization. There was only one sure way out of this. Only one way to finally be free. Only one way to finally be at peace.

Death.

CHAPTER 8

As planned, Jillian's mom had left for her workshop in Chicago yesterday morning, and as expected, last night, right after Jillian had spent a couple of hours watching Nickelodeon with Layla, and Layla had dropped off to sleep, her father had wasted no time coming into her room. It had simply been the worst, because he'd seemed so relaxed and so not in a hurry. She guessed because he didn't have to be.

First, he'd made her take off every stitch of clothing and lie flat on her back, and then he'd shot one photo after another. He'd even made her pose in different positions, the same way the photographers did on *America's Next Top Model,* except Jillian hadn't had anything on. Then, when he'd finished with that, he'd touched every body part she'd been born with and made her give him oral sex. Which was beyond nause-ating, because for the first time, he'd made her swallow this white, strong-tasting fluid, which she now knew was semen. She'd always wondered why, over the past month, after he made all those strange noises, he quickly pulled away from her, continued making strange noises, and wrapped himself inside a huge towel. But now that this nasty stuff was in her system, she'd been scared crazy about the possibility of being pregnant, because last year, her sex education teacher had explained the whole process. She'd told them that the way a man got a woman pregnant was when his sperm attached to one or more of her eggs. Jillian had been frightened beyond sanity until she'd searched the Internet this morning and learned that pregnancy wasn't possible by mouth.

Now it was Tuesday, and Jillian wondered why God wasn't hearing her. She wondered why He wasn't answering her prayers, why He wouldn't free her from all the pain she was enduring. Especially since with every week, she'd become more and more depressed. So much so that she'd changed her mind about spending the weekend with her grandparents. The plan had been that she and Nikki both would, but Jillian hadn't wanted them asking her any questions. She hadn't wanted them seeing that something was very wrong with her.

As far as school was concerned, she no longer enjoyed it, didn't talk much to any of her friends, not even Nikki, and she hadn't done homework or studied for a test in almost a month. Her grades were falling at an alarming rate and just this afternoon, she'd seen two letters from her school, addressed to her mother. She knew, without reading them, that they were outlining her new and very unusual lack of interest in her education.

She felt so completely defeated and had sat for days on end contemplating various ways to end her life. She had heard of people mixing different medications and then overdosing, people shooting themselves, people hanging themselves, and a number of other ways to do it, so what she had to do was figure out which would be the easiest and fastest way to go — that is, if she could get over the fact that deep down, she really didn't want to die. Well, actually, there was a tiny part of her that really did want to, sort of, so for the most part, she was extremely confused.

The phone rang and her father yelled for her to pick it up.

It was her mother.

"Hi, sweetie."

"Hi, Mom."

"How are you?"

"Okay."

"Honey, what's wrong? Because you don't sound like you're okay."

"Nothing."

"Jill, remember what I told you a few weeks ago? That you can tell me anything?"

Jillian burst into tears, weeping uncontrollably.

"Sweetie, what is it? Please tell me what's going on. You've really got me worried."

Jillian wept loudly and then saw her father enter her room, glaring at her in a disapproving way.

He walked over and took the phone from her.

"Baby, everything is fine. It's nothing serious. Jillian is just upset because a couple of letters came from the school today. They were addressed to you, but since you were gone and we never receive letters from school about Jillian, I figured I'd better open them. But even after I read them, I didn't want to bother you with this until you got back."

Jillian couldn't hear what her mom was saying, but then she heard her father say, "Her grades are falling, and she's skipped some of her classes more than once over the last four weeks. But I'll have a talk with her, and there's nothing for you to worry about. Everything will be fine. Jillian probably thought you were going to be angry with her, and I'll let her know that you're not."

He paused again while her mother was speaking and then said, "Yeah, she's still right here."

Her father gave her the phone back.

"Jill, why are your grades dropping?"

"I don't know. My classes are a lot harder this year, and I can't keep up." She hated lying to her mother, but she had to tell her something.

"But you've been a straight-A student since first grade."

Jillian didn't comment.

"We'll talk about this more when I get home tomorrow, and if we need to, we'll even hire a tutor for the subjects you need help with. But is that all this is about or is there something else? Because if it is something else, I want you to tell me. Remember, I told you, bad or good. I'm your mother, and it's my job to make sure you're okay. Make sure you're happy."

It took her a few seconds, but Jillian finally said, "No. There's nothing else wrong."

"Well, you be good, and I'll see you tomorrow."

"I love you, Mom."

"I love you, too."

When she hung up the phone, her father sat down in her desk chair.

"Jillian, I have to tell you that Daddy isn't very happy about your grades or about the way you've been missing classes. I'm also not happy about the way you cried on the phone to your mother, making her think something bad had happened to you. I know you don't quite understand why, but no matter what, you can never tell your mother or anyone else about our secret. I know you don't always agree, but you and I are not doing anything wrong. What we do together is very normal and you can bet all your little girlfriends are doing the same kinds of things with their fathers, but they just don't talk about it. They just know how to keep a secret, and that's the most important thing of all."

Jillian wondered how many more times he was going to try to convince her that what they were doing was "normal," but mostly she just wished he'd leave her room and never come back.

"You can also bet that other girls are enjoying every minute of the special times they have with their fathers, and I want you to start enjoying it, too. It will make me so much happier if you could be just as excited about it as I am."

Jillian wasn't sure how much more she could take of this, but she felt a little relieved when her father stood up and seemed to be heading toward her door. She frowned, however, when she saw him pull open one side of her closet and pull out a hot-pink, two-piece nightie that looked like the kind she'd seen in her mom's Victoria's Secret catalog. She'd gone in her closet herself, right after school, but she hadn't even noticed it.

"Here. I bought this for you earlier today, and I want you to put it on."

"No! I'm not doing that, and if you don't get out of my room, I'm calling Grandma and Grandpa."

"Have you forgotten that your grandparents are out of town? Have you forgotten that you asked your mom if you could stay with them while she was gone, and that's why you couldn't? I'll tell you something else, too. Carter told me a long time ago that he and your grandmother were going away this week, so when your mom told me about her workshop, I knew this would be a very special two or three days for you and me."

"Then, I'll call them on their cell phones.

Because I don't care what happens to me anymore, and I'm also telling Mom everything you've been making me do as soon as she gets home tomorrow."

"They'll all blame you. And you'll be out of this family for good. You'll be out on the street in no time."

"I don't care about that either. I'm still telling."

Jillian didn't know if she really could or not, but even if all her threats turned out to be nothing more than a bluff, she could tell she'd gotten his attention. She could see a bit of fear in his eyes, and she was somewhat relieved.

But sadly, he left her room and returned with his digital camera.

"Look," he said, shoving it in front of her. "Do you see these pictures?"

He flipped proudly through those disgusting photos he'd taken last night.

"Look at that huge smile on your face. Look how happy you look. So, do you think your mother or your grandparents are going to believe that you did this against your will?"

"But you made me smile, and that's the only reason I did. You told me that if I pretended like I was happy in a couple of the photos, you wouldn't take any more of them."

"But if you force me, I'll have to deny all of that. I'll have to tell your mother that you made me take those photos and that the reason I had no choice was because you said if I didn't take them, you'd tell her I tried to rape you. I'll tell her that I was so afraid she might believe you that I did what you demanded."

"What?! But I never said anything like that. You're the one who made *me* do everything. You've been making me do all kinds of nasty stuff ever since I was seven years old, Daddy. Ever since the day Layla was born."

"But that's always been our little secret, hasn't it? And the first thing your mother and your grandparents are going to want to know is why it took you five whole years to come to them. They're going to want to know why you let it go on this long, and then they'll realize that the reason you didn't say anything was because none of what you're claiming is true. They'll never believe one little thing ever happened between us."

Jillian picked up the pink nightie and threw it at him. She wasn't sure where she'd gotten the courage to do it, but she was glad she had. "Please, get out."

To her surprise, he left and didn't come back.

After a couple of hours had passed, Jillian thought about going into Layla's room to kiss her good night, but she was kind of afraid to leave her own. She certainly didn't want to run into her father, so she decided it was best to try to sleep instead.

"God, please just help me make it through the night and all of tomorrow without him bothering me again."

Jillian lay across her bed, closed her eyes, and couldn't wait for her mother to get home.

She was finally going to tell her everything.

She would tell, her mother would throw her father out, and she, her mother, and little Layla would be fine.

CHAPTER 9

Jillian hadn't been able to concentrate on anything her teachers had said today, and she was glad to finally be home. She was also happy her father still wasn't there yet because she wanted to think more about how she was going to start this long-overdue conversation with her mother. For hours now, she'd been trying to decide on what she would say and how she would say it. Mostly, though, she replayed her mother's words. *You can tell me anything, bad or good. It's my job to make sure you're okay.* She replayed those words and for the first time in weeks, she felt almost joyous and excited.

Jillian really believed her mom, and now she wished she'd told her a long time ago. Her mother had always shielded and protected her, well before her father had come into the picture, so she wasn't sure why she'd been so afraid to tell her the truth.

But it would all be over soon. When her

mother had called this morning, she'd told Jillian that the workshop would end around five, but with rush-hour traffic, she probably wouldn't make it back to Mitchell until around seven or eight. Which was fine because it was already six, anyway.

After an hour passed, Jillian tried focusing on her homework, but when she realized she'd read the same page in her history book three different times, she closed it and turned on the television. Layla walked in five minutes later and jumped onto her bed.

"What are you up to, little girl?"

"I'm not a little girl," she whined playfully. "I'm a big girl."

"Yeah, I guess you are. You're smart as a big girl, anyway."

"Yep."

"So, what did you do in school today?"

"We worked on some new three-letter words and then we finger-painted."

"Well, that sounds pretty messy."

"It was, and it was fun, too."

"I'll bet."

Layla held out her hands. "See? Some of it is still there because it was kinda hard washing it all off."

"It's pretty faint, so it'll be gone once you take your bath."

"Can we watch Disney?"

"Don't you ever get tired of that?"

"Nope. Disney and Nickelodeon are my two favorite channels, and all the kids in my class like them, too."

Jillian passed her baby sister the remote. "I'm sure."

"Thanks, Jill," she said, smiling. "You're the best big sister ever, and I love you sooooo much."

"I love you, too, Layla."

"Oh, and once we get to bring our finger-paint picture home, I'm going to let you have it."

"Well, that'll be nice."

"I like making stuff for you."

"I know, and I love when you give it to me, too."

Layla rolled onto her stomach and rested her chin inside her hands, and Jillian pulled out her journal. First, she flipped through and read what she'd written yesterday and the day before, and then she wrote about what she was going to be doing when her mother finally arrived home tonight. Suddenly, though, she wondered why her father was so quiet and hadn't said one word to her. He'd made more threats that morning, before she'd left on her way to school, but that had basically been it. Whatever his reason for keeping his distance, though, she was happy about it.

Another hour passed and Jillian heard her father outside her door.

"Layla, it's time to get ready for bed."

"Daddyyy, just a few more minutes. My show just came on."

"I'm sorry, pumpkin. You know Mommy likes you to be in bed by eight, and it's already eight oh one."

"Okayyyy. Good night, Jill," she said, hugging her.

"Good night, little sister."

Jillian watched Layla as she left the room and then searched for something to watch on television. She stopped when she saw a young girl, who was maybe seven or eight, crying and standing between two women.

Jillian listened, and it wasn't long before she heard the child say, "Daddy's been touching me down here, Mommy." Jillian couldn't believe what she was hearing, but the girl continued. "Mommy, he's been hurting me."

The little girl was very upset, but what stunned Jillian were the words she heard the girl's mother say next. "Just shut up, Kerri! Stop telling all these vicious lies." Then Kerri's mom shook her daughter until the other woman pulled her away from her.

"Doctor, she's lying, I tell you. I don't

know why, but she's telling a bald-faced lie. My husband would never do such a horrible thing."

"Mrs. Anderson, I've only counseled with Kerri on two other occasions, but I'm not surprised by what she's saying."

The mother scowled. "And what exactly is that supposed to mean?"

"That I knew she was keeping a very painful secret. I just had this feeling about it, and today she told me everything and I told her we had to tell you as well."

"I don't care what she says, she's a filthy little liar! Kerri, why are you doing this? Don't you want Mommy to be happy? Do you want Daddy to have to go away? Do you want to go back to having no father at all?"

Kerri looked dumbfounded and didn't speak.

"Well, if you don't, then you'd better stop making up all of these outlandish stories. Do you hear me?" Mrs. Anderson yelled, grabbing both her daughter's arms and shaking her. "I said, do you hear me?"

"Yes, Mommy," she said between deep sniffles, her body heaving.

Mrs. Anderson yanked Kerri's arm and dragged her out of the office. But before they disappeared out of sight, the doctor hurried to the doorway and called out to the mother. "Mrs. Anderson, just so you know, by law, I have no choice but to report this to the Division of Children and Family Services."

Jillian watched Mrs. Anderson storm out of the building without looking back and then the movie went to a commercial break. *This just couldn't be,* was all Jillian could think. Had her father been right all along? Had he not been simply trying to manipulate her? Had he really been telling the truth after all? *Your mother will blame you for everything, and she'll kick you out of the house for good. Our entire family will be ruined, it'll be all your fault, and everyone will hate you from now on.* Would her mother yell at her the same way Mrs. Anderson had just yelled at little Kerri?

Jillian wasn't sure, but there was no way she could chance the outcome. If she did and things didn't turn out favorably, where would she go? Who would take care of her? Her father had already insisted that her grandparents would be just as angry with her, and since her mother was an only child, it wasn't like she had any aunts or uncles she could turn to. Her only option would be foster care, and she couldn't see risking that either, because she'd heard her mom mentioning far too many foster-parent horror stories. Then there were the lies her father had sworn he would tell about her. If he did, what would everyone think of her? What if Nikki and the rest of her schoolmates heard about what she'd been doing? And what about all the people she knew at church?

So, no, she couldn't tell her mother anything. She'd just have to pretend that everything was okay and then promise to get her grades back up to where they used to be. She would pretend like never before that she simply couldn't be happier, and then she would wait to see if God was finally going to answer her prayers and put an end to this very sad and disgraceful life she was living. She would wait, because as of a few moments ago, when she'd heard her father summoning her sweet, innocent little sister, she'd come to an undeniable realization: Dying was no longer one of her options. Dying was no longer possible because if she killed herself, who would her father prey on next?

The answer was obvious, and it was the reason she could no longer feel sad, depressed, or like she couldn't go on, even if she wanted to. She could no longer focus on herself because Layla's safety was far more important.

CHAPTER 10

Over the last three weeks, Jillian had been all smiles, and as it had turned out, she no longer had to pretend about anything. For the first time in a long time, she really was pretty happy, and it was all because her father had changed for the better. He'd even apologized for taking all those photos, and he never approached her in the wrong kind of way, even when they were in the house by themselves. She wasn't sure why exactly, but she had a feeling that her standing up to him and then threatening to tell her mother what he'd been doing was the reason. He'd never brought that whole evening up to her again, and he acted as though they had the ideal family — like they were no different from the flawless families on some of the TV shows she'd seen — like they'd never had any major problems or issues, one way or another.

Which was fine with Jillian, because she

was now getting perfect scores again on her homework assignments and tests, she was participating full force in all of her extracurricular activities, and she'd even been talking to Kyle on the phone again every night. Her mother still wouldn't let him visit her, insisting that Jillian was much too young to receive boy company, but Jillian spent as much time with him as she could at school.

"I literally can't wait to get to the dance tomorrow night," Nikki exclaimed while sitting at her maple desk, polishing her fingernails.

Jillian sat Indian style on top of Nikki's queen-size bed, skimming the latest issue of *CosmoGirl* magazine. "I hope it's a lot better than the one we went to earlier this month, because to be honest, that one really wasn't all that exciting."

Nikki turned around and looked at her. "That's because you didn't know how to make it exciting and because you were still acting like you didn't want to be bothered with Kyle. Girl, dances are only fun if you have a boy to hang out with."

"You crack me up. But anyway, what are you planning to wear?"

"My jean jumper skirt that comes just above the knee and the jacket that goes with it."

"Well, I'm wearing pants because it's too cold to be wearing any dress or skirt. I'll probably wear some black leggings and my orange sweater that hangs toward the middle of my thighs."

"Being cold will be the least of my worries, and plus it's only the end of October, so it's not like it's winter."

"It's still really chilly outside at night, though, and what do you mean it will be the least of your worries?"

Nikki smiled slyly.

"What?"

"There's something I've been wanting to tell you for three days now."

"And?"

"Remember on Monday when I told you I couldn't volunteer at the nursing home because I had to meet with my math teacher? And that my mom couldn't pick us up right after school that day anyway to take us because she had an appointment?"

"Yeah?"

"Well, that wasn't really the truth."

They normally didn't lie to each other, so Jillian wondered what this was all about. "Then where were you?"

"I went home with Marcus, and we had sex for the first time."

Jillian was stunned. "Oh my God. Where

were his parents?"

"They were upstairs for a while, but then they left. Marcus's room is on the lower level, so after we came in and spoke to them, we never saw them again."

"They left you there all by yourselves?"

"Yep. His parents are so, so neat, and Marcus said they never trip out like a lot of parents do."

"So, how did you get home?"

"My mom."

"What?!"

"Marcus called his older cousin who's in the twelfth grade, and he dropped me back off at school and then I called my mom to pick me up."

"Wow. Weren't you afraid of getting caught?"

"No, and my mom never suspected a thing."

"So, what was it like? And were you nervous?"

"Yes. Very nervous, and at first, it hurt really bad. But then it got better once he got it all the way in and we kept doing it. I was sore, though, pretty much every day except today."

"Unreal. So, did you like it? I mean, would you do it again?"

"Definitely, girl. And actually that's why

I'm so looking forward to the dance tomorrow, because Marcus and I are planning to sneak out of it."

"To go where?"

"Somewhere behind the school and up in these bushes he was telling me about."

"In some bushes? As cold as it is?"

"Girl, I already told you, I'm not worried about what the weather is going to be like, and I guarantee you Marcus isn't either. We just want to be together."

"I guess."

"Plus Marcus is going to stash a big blanket and a couple of pillows inside this garbage bag, so we'll be fine."

"Man. I can't believe you're not a virgin anymore. I can't believe you actually did it with him."

"When we finished, it was hard for me to believe, too, but now I'm glad I did because now Marcus knows that I'm for real and that he's not dealing with some scared little girl."

Jillian kept quiet because she knew she fell right into that same "scared little girl" category and had no intention of having sex any time soon.

"There's also something else I didn't tell you."

"What?"

"Right after Marcus and I started going together, he taught me how to give him oral sex. And, girl, he now says that no other girl has ever done it nearly as well as I can."

Jillian couldn't help thinking about her father and all the times he'd made her do the same thing, but she quickly pushed all of that from her mind.

"I didn't like it in the beginning," Nikki continued. "But then when I saw how much Marcus enjoyed having it done to him, it made me like it a whole lot more."

Jillian wasn't sure what she should say, so she turned one of the pages in the magazine she was still holding.

"And you know, Jill, you need to think about doing the same thing. Because even if you don't want to have real sex with Kyle, at least you could do the oral thing for him."

"Kyle hasn't even mentioned sex to me."

"But you know he's eventually going to, because all boys have to have it. It's just the way things are, and if you want to keep him interested, you're going to have to find a way to satisfy him."

Jillian shook her head and flipped another page.

"Okay, girl. You'd better listen to me before some other girl gives Kyle exactly what he needs."

"It's not like we're girlfriend and boyfriend, anyway, so I'm not even thinking about that."

"But you know it's only a matter of time before he officially asks you to be his girl."

"We don't know that."

"*I* know it, because Marcus already gave me the four-one-one. He also told me that Kyle has wanted to ask you for a while but then you went through whatever it was you were going through and wouldn't talk to him."

Jillian could barely contain herself. Kyle really wanted her to be his girl. She couldn't have been happier, but there was one thing she hoped Nikki was dead wrong about: that he would soon want her to have sex with him. Even oral sex wasn't something she was willing to do, because just the thought of letting Kyle put his thing in her mouth was enough to make her ill. Just the thought of oral sex, period, reminded her of her father and sent cold chills running through her. What she hoped was that Kyle would continue being the nice boy he seemed to be and not at all like Marcus.

Nikki closed her polish bottle, but her face turned serious. "Can I ask you something, Jill?"

"Yeah, go ahead."

"What was up with you last month? I mean, I know I've asked you this before, but why did you just cut me off the way you did? You wouldn't talk to me at school, you wouldn't talk to me on the phone, and if we're supposed to be best friends, then I don't understand why you can't tell me. You cut everyone off, you stopped doing all our extracurricular stuff, and you seemed so sad."

Jillian wished Nikki would stop bringing this up and would just forget it ever happened. Life was finally good for Jillian at home now, and she didn't want to think about all the times when it hadn't been. What she wanted was to put every bit of that behind her and move on.

"It was just some weird phase I went through. I'm not sure why, but it's over now and I'm fine."

"Did I do something to cause it?"

"No. Not at all."

"Did someone else do something to you?"

"No." Jillian's tone was short. "I told you, it was just some phase that I can't explain. It just happened, all right?"

"Well, it's not like you have to get so upset about it. I'm only asking because I was really worried about you, and I was afraid for you."

"Afraid of what?"

"I don't know. That maybe somebody was hurting you. At least that's what Ashley and Shelly were worried about, anyway, and that made me worry, too."

Jillian tossed the magazine she'd been reading onto the bed. "Hurting me how?"

Nikki hunched her shoulders. "How am I supposed to know? They were just worried, and right before you started talking to me again, we were gonna ask you about it. But then we saw that you were happy again and acting like your old self."

"Well, all three of you were worrying for nothing."

"I know that now, but when you wouldn't talk to me, I didn't know what to think."

Jillian picked up the magazine and ignored Nikki's last comment. Now she wondered what everyone else at school had been thinking, too. She'd done a fabulous job of pretending to be happy whenever she was home, making sure her mother didn't notice at all how depressed she was, and now she wished she'd put on the same facade at school. But she'd become so tired of putting on like everything was okay, all day long, and finally when her father had resorted to taking photos of her naked body and had continued forcing himself inside her mouth, she'd broken down emotionally, and school was the place she'd chosen to let her true feelings show.

Nikki turned back around, facing her desk, and unscrewed a bottle of topcoat. Thankfully, she didn't say anything else on the subject, and Jillian hoped that would be the case from now on, because what she wanted was to put that miserable chapter of her life behind her. It was over, and she didn't want to dwell on it or think about it again.

CHAPTER 11

Jillian's mom sat an oblong pan of fried chicken onto the laminated, light oak dining room table and then followed with a dish of creamed corn and warm, buttered dinner rolls. Jillian brought in a glass pitcher of homemade iced tea, and the two of them took their seats. Her father and Layla had been sitting and waiting for the last ten minutes or so, and they were finally ready for him to say grace.

"Dear Heavenly Father, we come right now just thanking you for another day. We thank you for our beautiful and very loving family and for all that you have so graciously given us. We thank you for the food we are about to receive and for meeting our every single need. In Your son Jesus's name, Amen."

Jillian, her mom, and Layla spoke in unison. "Amen."

Her father lifted a pair of steel tongs and

placed two wings and a breast on his plate. "So, I hear there's a school dance tomorrow night."

"There is, and it's supposed to be the biggest one of the year."

Jillian's mom spooned out a sizable helping of corn. "I tell you, it seems like forever since I was in junior high and couldn't wait to go to all our dances. We would have the time of our lives. Learning and doing all the new dance steps. It was so much fun, and those definitely were the days."

"I remember how fun it was, too," her father said. "But I also remember how the chaperones had to keep their eyes on most of the boys, making sure they stayed in line and weren't trying to do things they weren't supposed to."

Her mom chuckled. "I remember that at my school, too, and I also remember them having to keep on some of those fast little girls."

Her father poured himself some tea. "I know. But that's where we're very blessed, because our little princess isn't like that. She's not thinking about any of these little thickhead boys in the least. Right, princess?"

Jillian hated lying, but she knew it was best to say exactly what she knew her father wanted to hear. "That's right. I just like hanging out with Nikki, Ashley, and Shelly and dancing to all the new songs."

"But what about that boy, Kyle, who's been calling here?" her father asked, and she wished he'd stop forcing her to be so dishonest.

"Kyle is nothing but a good friend of mine. No different than Nikki. We're just friends because we both know we're too young to be boyfriend and girlfriend. We're not even thinking about anything like that."

Her father looked at her and then back down at his plate, and she couldn't tell whether he'd bought her story or not.

Her mother smiled, though. "You know, sweetie, I probably don't tell you this enough, but I couldn't have asked for a better daughter. Or I guess I should say *we* couldn't have asked for a better daughter, because I know your father feels the same way. You've always been the model child and always so mindful and respectful of what your elders tell you to do. You've always paid attention to what's good for you and what isn't, and you've never been disobedient like so many other children are. We're so proud of you, Jill."

"Thanks, Mom."

"We definitely are," her father added. "More proud than you could ever know."

"But what about me?" Layla whined. "Because I'm your daughter, too."

Everyone laughed, and then their mother said, "Oh, honey, of course you are. We're very proud of you, too, and you never give us any trouble either. We love both you and Jill more than anything in this world."

Layla smiled with satisfaction and ate a piece of her roll. Jillian bit a piece of her drumstick.

"So, is Nikki's mom still going to drop you guys off tomorrow night?" her mother asked.

"I think so."

"That'll work well, then, because your dad and I made reservations at that new Mexican restaurant near the mall."

Layla looked at her mom. "Does that I mean I get to go with Jill?"

"No, honey, you're going to go over to your grandparents'."

"But why? Why can't I go with Jill to the big dance?"

"Because it's only for the kids who go to Jill's school."

Layla folded her arms and pouted. "I never get to do anything."

"Of course you do, pumpkin," her father said. "You get to do a lot of fun stuff all the time."

"But I don't get to go anywhere with Jill and her friends."

"That's because you're not old enough yet. But you'll get there, and before long, you'll be going to your own dances at your own junior high school."

Layla didn't say anything else, but Jillian could tell she still wasn't happy. She'd be fine, though, once she arrived at their grandparents', because they always let Layla eat and do whatever she wanted. They always let her rule the house completely whenever she came over, the same as they'd done with Jillian when she was that age.

After Jillian and her mom had cleared the table and loaded everything into the dishwasher, Jillian went upstairs and called Kyle. She had a lot of homework to do, but she didn't want to miss talking to him for at least a few minutes. Interestingly enough, a few minutes turned into thirty.

"You know I can't wait to dance with you, don't you?" he said.

"Yes."

"And I hope your girls don't mind, because I want you to be with me the whole three hours."

"They'll be fine."

"I'm just making sure, because you know how much you guys like to stick together."

"Well, we already know Nikki's going to be with Marcus the whole night, anyway."

"That we do, because Marcus has been bragging about it to the entire team all this week."

Jillian was mortified. "Oh my God. He's been telling people about him and Nikki sneaking out of the dance tomorrow night?"

"Of course he has. He also told us when he got it from her for the first time, too. He tells on all the girls he does it with. That's just the way Marcus is."

"He is so wrong for that."

"Maybe, but if I were you, I would advise Nikki not to sneak anywhere with Marcus. Especially not up in those woods."

"Why?"

Kyle paused and then spoke. "Look, all I'm saying is that Marcus can't be trusted, and Nikki had better stop while she's ahead. I mean, I don't want you telling her that I said any of this, but you need to let her know that Marcus is planning to use her big time tomorrow night, and then he's going to dump her. He's been saying all week how tired he is of her and that he's already got his eye on someone else."

"I told her to leave him alone in the first place. I practically begged her because I never liked him. I knew he was bad news and that Nikki was going to get her feelings hurt. But she wouldn't listen to me."

"Well, she'd better listen to you now, because if Marcus says he's going to do something, that's exactly what he means."

"I'd better get off so I can try to call her."

"Remember what I said about not mentioning my name."

"I won't."

"Okay, then, I'll let you go."

"See you in the morning."

Jillian pressed the end button and dialed Nikki's number.

"Hey, Jill, what's up?"

"Not much. What's up with you?"

"Just trying on my outfit I'm wearing to the dance. Then I have some math to work on. Actually, girl, I'm surprised you're not doing homework yourself, because by this time of night, that's all you're usually thinking about," she said, teasing her and laughing.

"I know, but there's something I really need to talk about."

Jillian couldn't believe all the lies she'd had to tell this evening. *God, please forgive me. But I have to find a way to warn Nikki.* "I was walking down the hallway at school and overheard some guys talking about you and Marcus."

"So what? People talk all the time."

"But this was different."

"Different how?"

"They were saying that Marcus was going to take you in those woods and use you big time and then he was going to dump you. Then they said he was already tired of you and that he had his eye on some other girl."

"Yeah, right. Marcus would never say anything like that, and to prove it, he just told me an hour ago that he's in love with me."

"But it sounded like everything they were saying was true, Nik."

"Please. And anyway, those guys you heard were probably only saying those things because *they* can't get with me. They're just mad because they know they don't have a chance."

"Nikki, you know I always had a bad feeling about Marcus, so please don't leave with him tomorrow night."

"Honey, our plans are already set, and there's no way on earth I'm disappointing Marcus. So stop worrying."

"But, Nik, I believe every single thing I heard. I mean, why would someone make up something like that? And how did they know you and Marcus were going to be sneaking out of the dance in the first place?

So you know he had to at least tell that much of it."

"Wow. I can't believe you're taking all these lies so seriously."

"But that's just it. I don't think they *are* lies. I think there's a lot of truth to it."

"You know what? Maybe the real problem is you."

"What?"

"You heard me. Maybe you're just as jealous as those pathetic little wimps you overheard, only you're jealous for a different reason. Maybe the big problem here is that you wish you were the one Marcus had chosen to be with. Or maybe you're just mad because Kyle hasn't asked you to have sex with him the way Marcus asked me."

"That's not true, Nikki, and you know it."

"No, I don't know anything. Because if you were really my friend the way you claim to be, you would just be happy for me."

"Why can't you ever listen to anybody?"

"I'm not listening because you're talkin' a bunch of silly junk. And it's like I said: I think you're just upset because Kyle doesn't want to have sex with you. There's probably something wrong with his little boring behind, anyway. He's probably afraid to even touch a girl in that kind of way."

"Why are you being so cruel? Especially

when I'm only trying to stop you from getting hurt."

"What you need to do is mind your own business," she said, and hung up the phone.

Jillian set her cordless onto its base and felt like crying. In all the years they'd been friends, not once had Nikki said such hurtful words to her, and Jillian could barely remember them having any real arguments. They disagreed on certain things — well, a lot of things for that matter — but they never got angry enough to hang up on each other the way Nikki had just now.

Jillian so wished she could get through to her. Make her see what a huge jerk Marcus was and that, from the very beginning, he had only wanted one thing from her. Make her see that all the rumors about him weren't really rumors at all and that everything Jillian had heard about him was true.

She wished that somehow she could just get her to see that being with him was an enormous mistake.

But she knew all of the above was completely out of the question because Nikki was going to be Nikki. She was going to do whatever she pleased, and she didn't care what anyone had to say about it.

Chapter 12

Miss G turned into the school parking lot and slowed down her vehicle. Cars, SUVs, trucks, and vans were everywhere, and kids were getting out of them and saying good-bye to their parents, one after another. Some had come to the dance alone and were probably going to meet up with their friends inside, and some had carpooled the same as Jillian and Nikki. Although it really didn't feel like the two of them had ridden together at all, because Nikki still wasn't speaking to Jillian. She hadn't spoken to her all day in school, and until Miss G had pulled into their driveway and honked, Jillian hadn't been all that sure they were still going to pick her up tonight. She was sure Miss G had no idea that they'd had such a terrible argument, but she wasn't sure if maybe Nikki was so angry that she might tell her mom that Jillian wasn't go-ing. She'd been worried that Nikki might tell her anything, just so she didn't have to deal with her.

Miss G drove up a few feet, pressed on her brakes again, and then looked at Nikki. "Are you girls okay?"

"We're fine," Nikki hurried to say.

"Jillian?" Miss G turned around and asked.

"Everything's fine."

"Well, it sure doesn't seem like it. You girls haven't said two words to each other since we left Jillian's house."

Jillian wished she could tell Miss G what the problem was, so that maybe she could talk some sense into Nikki, but she knew she could never do that. She knew Nikki would hate her from then on and would never speak to her again.

Finally, after another few minutes, Miss G drove directly in front of the entrance. "You girls be good and have fun."

Jillian opened the back door. "Thanks for the ride, Miss G."

"Any time."

Nikki kissed her mom on the cheek. "See you later, Mom."

"See you when you get home."

Jillian and Nikki closed their respective doors and started toward the building, but

Jillian couldn't take this silent business any longer.

"Nikki, wait. I'm really sorry. I had no right trying to tell you what to do, and I really should have just minded my own business."

Nikki stopped and looked at her. "I'm sorry, too, and it killed me not being able to talk to you all day. Let's not ever let that happen again, okay?"

"Okay," she said, and they hugged each other.

"I really am going to be fine, though, girl. You'll see."

Jillian smiled and hoped this would end up being the case.

In the cafeteria, all the tables and chairs were moved against the walls, and one of Rihanna's singles was playing pretty loudly. The room was crowded, but Jillian could tell that Nikki was already scanning the room for Marcus. So far, he didn't seem to be anywhere in sight, and Jillian wished he wouldn't show up at all.

But so much for wishes, hopes, and dreams.

"Hey, you," Marcus said to Nikki, and then stood beside her and locked his fingers inside hers. Then he said, "Hey, Jill."

"Hi."

"Your boy went to the restroom . . . oh, here he comes now."

Jillian turned and saw Kyle coming toward them.

"Hey," he said when he walked in front of her.

"Hey."

"So, did you guys just get here?"

"Yep. A few minutes ago."

"Cool. That DJ is bumpin'."

"I know."

The four of them stood and listened to the next song being played, one of Usher's, but before it ended, Nikki pulled Jillian to the side.

"I'm out of here, girl. See you when I see you."

Jillian wanted to plead with her one last time, but she knew it was no use. Although there was one bright side to all of this. If Kyle was right about Marcus planning to have sex with Nikki one last time and then dump her, that would mean Nikki wouldn't have to worry about him hurting her again. Of course, she would be hurt this one time, but Jillian would help her get through the whole breakup and that would be the end of it.

When Nikki and Marcus slipped out of the cafeteria, Kyle took Jillian's hand. "Do you wanna dance?"

"Okay," she told him, and felt her hand sort of trembling, because a slow song was playing. Although at least the DJ seemed to have turned the volume down quite a bit. She'd danced a number of times with boys on fast songs but never a slow one, and she could only imagine what her father would say if he found out about it.

"I really do like you a lot, Jill," he said as soon as they took their first couple of steps.

She wanted to respond but couldn't find the words.

"Did you hear me?"

"Yes."

"And you really like me, too, right?"

"Yes."

"Well, that's why I've been thinking about something all week, but I don't know how you're going to feel about it."

Jillian's nerves radiated, and she didn't like the sound of what he'd said. *What if he now wants me to have sex with him?* "What is it?"

"Are you sure you want to hear it?"

"Why wouldn't I? Is it something bad?"

"No. I think it's something good."

"Then tell me."

"Okay, here goes. I've been thinking about what it would feel like to kiss you and if you'd be okay with me doing it."

"Oh."

"So, what do you think?"

"I don't know."

"It will only be a kiss, and that's all. Nothing else, because I can tell you're not ready for anything more than that and I would never ask you to do something you don't wanna do. But I do want to kiss you, and I also want something else."

"What?"

"For you to be my girl."

Jillian tried to stop herself from smiling too much and was glad he was tall enough that her face rested close to his shoulder and he couldn't see her expression.

"So, will you?"

"Yes."

"Good. And is it also okay for us to kiss?"

"Not in here."

"No, outside on the side of the building when the dance is almost over."

"Okay."

They danced the next three songs straight, and Jillian had never been more excited about anything. This was, by far, the best night of her life, and she couldn't wait to see what it felt like to kiss someone she really liked. Someone her own age. A boy and not a grown man.

Finally, after dancing to a few more songs and then sitting and chatting for a while, Jillian looked at her watch and got a little nervous. Nikki and Marcus still weren't back yet. She was nervous because she knew her parents were going to be there right on time, and that would be in about twenty minutes.

"My mom and dad are going to be here soon," she said.

"Then let's leave now."

On the way to the cafeteria exit, Jillian waved good-bye to Ashley and Shelly, and she and Kyle made their way outside and around to a lighted corner. It was really chilly, and she was glad Kyle had immediately wrapped his arms around her waist. She wrapped hers around his neck, and he kissed her. At first, Jillian sort of liked the way it felt and closed her eyes, but then when he switched from regular kissing to tongue kissing, she experienced awful flashbacks. She saw her father's face and pulled away from Kyle.

But Kyle pulled her back toward him and started kissing her again. She tried her best to bear it, but she couldn't. No matter how hard she tried. He kissed her, but without even realizing it, she pushed him with so much force that he fell to the ground. "I can't do this," she yelled.

She could tell he was gravely confused and didn't understand.

"Why'd you do that? What's wrong with you?"

"Nothing. My parents are probably here, so we need to go."

"But why are you acting like this?"

"We really have to go. Please."

Kyle got up and brushed the dust from his jeans. "Whatever."

But when they made it back to the parking lot area, she wanted to vanish. Her father was standing outside of his SUV, watching her every move, and he didn't look happy. He was furious, and she knew it was because he'd seen her and Kyle walking from the side of the school. She became even more afraid when she didn't see her mother.

"What in the world were you doing back there? And who is this boy?" her father said.

"Um, this is Kyle. You know, the Kyle that calls me sometimes."

"Uh-huh, but what were the two of you doing around there all in the dark?"

"Nothing. We just walked back there to talk. We just came out of the dance a few minutes ago."

"Yeah, I'll bet."

"We did, Daddy. We really did."

"Get in the car! And where's Nikki?"

"I think she's still inside."

Kyle took a step backward. "Jill, I think that's my mom over there, so I'll call you tomorrow, okay?"

"No, I don't think so," her father declared.

Kyle looked just as frightened as Jillian was and hurried down the sidewalk.

"I'll go back in to get Nikki," she said, although something told her Nikki wasn't in there.

And she was right, because no sooner than when she'd turned around, she heard someone screaming and crying. To her regret, it was in fact Nikki, and she looked a mess. Her hair was all over her head, grass was scattered through parts of it, and her shirt and jean jumper were saturated with tons of dirt. When she'd left, she'd had on a jean jacket, too, but now it was nowhere to be found.

Nikki slowly strode toward Jillian and her father, and everyone in the parking lot stared and whispered.

"Oh my God, Nik, what happened to you?" Jillian said, embracing her.

"Nothing," she said, still sobbing. "I just want to go home."

"Did some boy do this to you?" Jillian's

father asked.

"No. Some girls jumped me. They jumped me from behind and for no reason."

"Well, where are they now?" Jillian asked.

Nikki moved away from Jillian and pulled open the back door of the SUV. "I don't know. But can we please leave here?"

"Maybe we should call the police and just wait for them," Jillian's father suggested.

"No, Mr. James. Please, please just take me home. I'm begging you."

Nikki got in, he closed the door behind her, and Jillian got in on the other side but in the back with Nikki. Her father drove away, but everyone was still standing and watching. Nikki cried uncontrollably, and Jillian pulled her best friend into her arms.

"Nik, who were these girls?"

"I don't know, and I don't wanna talk about it anymore. I just wanna go home to my mom."

Jillian wanted to ask more questions, but she didn't, and they drove the rest of the way in silence. When they arrived, they all got out and went up to the front door. Miss G must have heard them pull up because she opened the door right away.

"Oh my goodness, what happened?" she said, clearly upset.

Nikki and her mom grabbed hold of each

other, and Nikki cried even harder.

"Baby, what happened? Please tell me."

Jillian wondered if Nikki would give more details, but all she did was repeat the same thing, that some girls had jumped her. Although she did add some part about these mysterious girls asking her to come outside and that they'd lured her around back.

"You went with these girls, and you didn't even know them? And wasn't the dance just for the students who go there?"

"Yes, but they must have snuck in because I've never seen them before. And I only went outside with them because they seemed nice and were having a lot of fun."

Miss G looked at Jillian. "Is this true, Jill?"

Nikki quickly answered for her. "She was on the dance floor when I left with them, and that's why she didn't see anything."

"This is crazy," Miss G said. "And I'm calling the police."

"No, Mom. Please don't do that."

"Byron, if you don't mind, can you and Jill stay here until the police arrive?"

"We'll be glad to, and you're definitely doing the right thing by calling them. I don't understand why the chaperones at these dances allow kids to go out of the school before the dance is over anyway," he said, looking at Jillian, and she knew he was still livid about catching her with Kyle. "And I never saw even one security person, which they should assign outside the building at every school function, regardless of whether they have problems with violence or not."

When the two officers, one woman and one man, arrived, they questioned Nikki and then questioned Jillian, but Nikki still gave no additional information. She stuck to her story, and it was obvious that while the officers would file a report, there wasn't going to be a whole lot they could do without names or even some kind of physical description. Needless to say, Miss G was beside herself. She was angry at Nikki for leaving the dance with a bunch of girls she didn't know and hurt over the violent thing that had happened to her.

Finally, not long after the officers left, Jillian hugged Nikki and Miss G and told Nikki she'd be over to check on her tomorrow. Her father hugged both of them as well, and he and Jillian left.

But as soon as they did, her father tore into her about Kyle and drove like a madman.

"You really, really disappointed me tonight, and I had no idea you'd turned into such a little whore. I had no idea that all this time you've been having sex with that little boy."

"I'm not, Daddy. I haven't done anything with him."

"Shut up! You're such a big liar, and I should have known that as soon as you started talking to this boy on the phone, it was only going to be a matter of time before you let him have his way with you. You let him put it in you, didn't you?"

"No. I didn't. I wouldn't do that. We were only talking."

He slammed on the accelerator again. "You think I'm stupid, don't you?"

Jillian wondered where those police officers were now. "Oh God, Daddy, you're going to kill us."

"I thought you were my little princess, and that's why I've always tried to be everything I could to you."

"But I am, Daddy. I promise you, I haven't had sex with Kyle or any other boy. I wouldn't lie to you about that."

Jillian wasn't sure why, but for some reason, he slowed down and took a deep breath. "Even if you didn't do it with him, I'll bet you wanted to. And the thought of you being with any boy at all makes me crazy. I could never take you having special times with anyone the way you've had them with me."

Jillian kept quiet and prayed he would get her home safe and sound.

Her father looked straight ahead. "Did you kiss him?"

"No."

"If you lie to me again, I can't be responsible for what I might do. Now, tell me the truth."

"Okay, yes. I did kiss him, but I didn't like it. I didn't like it at all."

She waited for him to say something else, but he didn't. Not until they drove inside the garage and he switched off the ignition.

He then turned and faced her. "Thank you for being honest."

His mood had changed drastically, and even at twelve, Jillian knew this wasn't ordinary behavior.

"I'm sorry for doubting you, because deep down, I knew my princess could never give herself to some little punk, but I had to make sure. I had to make sure you hadn't turned into the same slutty little tramp your friend Nikki has turned into. Claiming she was jumped by a bunch of girls when she knows full well she was laid up in those woods with some no-good boy."

Jillian didn't dare say a word.

"And just so we don't have to worry about

this Kyle character trying to pressure you into doing something dirty and sinful again, I don't want him calling here anymore."

"But, Daddy —"

"Either that or I'm telling your mother what I caught you doing. I'll tell her that I caught you on the side of the school giving Mr. Kyle Davis a blow job. I'll tell her that you were doing it like a pro, and that this can only mean one thing — that you've obviously had a whole lot of practice with it."

Tears seeped from Jillian's eyes and down her face, but she quickly wiped them away.

"You'd better dry all of that up before we go inside, because if you don't, your mom is going to wanna know what's wrong with you. And she doesn't need that kind of worry, because Layla isn't feeling all that well. She came down with some sort of stomach flu when she was at your grandparents' and that's why your mom wanted to be dropped off at home with her before I came to pick you up. And now I'm glad she didn't come with me because she would have been just heartbroken if she'd seen you coming out of the dark with that little boy."

Jillian sniffled, got out of the car, and tried

figuring out who she should feel the sorriest for.

Nikki or herself.

Chapter 13

Jillian opened her eyes, awaking from a very deep sleep, and sighed. Last night had been a most eventful evening and one she prayed wouldn't repeat itself any time soon. Her father had acted like a stoned maniac and had abruptly turned back into the same monster he'd been all along. Things had been so much better over the last few weeks, but now that the evil in him had returned, Jillian wondered what this was going to mean for the two of them.

Then there was Nikki and her unpleasant and seemingly hostile incident, and the question of what had in fact really happened. She'd practically sworn to her story about these so-called girls beating her up, but for some reason, Jillian didn't believe it. She was almost sure Marcus had something to do with this, but there was no way she could prove it. Nikki had gladly left with him of her own free will, but something had gone terribly wrong. Plus, where had Marcus been when this posse of girls had confronted Nikki? Not to mention Nikki didn't have any scratches or bruises on her face, so that was even more reason not to believe the story she'd kept repeating.

Jillian left her bed, went over and opened her blinds, and stood there for a few moments, allowing the sun to shine across her face. She then picked up her cordless phone and dialed Nikki.

Miss G answered after the third ring. "Hello?"

"Hi, Miss G. How are you?"

"I'm fine, honey. How are you?"

"I'm good."

"You wanna speak to Nikki?"

"Yes, thank you."

Miss G must have been in the same room with her because Nikki got on right away. "Hi."

"Hey. How are you?"

"I'm fine. Everything is okay."

"I was so afraid for you."

"I was, too, but it's all over now and that's all that matters."

"I wish the police could find out who those girls were."

"I do, too, but there's no way they can because I didn't recognize any of them."

"Then why do you think they did that to you? Because normally when people want to fight, it's because they have some sort of issue with you."

"I don't know. But hey, I have to go now."

"Okay, but I'll be over this afternoon sometime."

"Thanks, Jill."

Jillian pressed the end button and wondered why Nikki was sticking to such an unbelievable lie. It didn't make any sense, but maybe she had a good reason for telling it.

Jillian looked up when she heard a knock at her door. "Come in."

It was her mother. "Good morning, sweetie."

"Good morning, Mom."

"You should probably call and check on Nikki. See how she's doing."

"I just hung up with her."

"Well, did she tell you anything different?"

Jillian had filled her mother in when she'd gotten home last night, but her mother had seemed just as puzzled as she was. "No. And we didn't stay on the phone very long. She seemed like she was in a hurry to get off."

"Mm, mm, mm. It's so sad, and I just don't understand it."

"Neither do I."

"I'm just glad you were smart enough not to leave the dance until it was completely over and it was time for you to come home."

Jillian knew that hadn't been the case, what with her going outside with Kyle, but she couldn't tell her mother that. She couldn't, and she hoped her father wouldn't tell on her either.

"You don't think some little boy did something to her, do you?"

"I don't know. When we saw her coming from the back of the school, she was by herself and we never saw anyone else."

"I don't think it's a good idea for you girls to go to any more of these dances."

Jillian didn't like the sound of that, because if she couldn't go to dances or other evening and weekend events, she'd never get to see Kyle outside of their regular school day. As it was, her father had already banned her from talking to him on the phone.

"Why?"

"Because it's much too dangerous, and the last thing I want is for something like this to happen to you. People are so crazy nowadays, and there's just no telling what they might do anymore."

"This has never happened before, though. Not at our school, and I doubt that it'll happen again."

"We'll see, but just the idea that something happened to Nikki last night is enough for us to be a lot more cautious. But like I said, we'll see."

"Are we still going to the grocery store?"

"Yes, and actually, I'm about to jump in the shower now."

"Can you drop me off at Nikki's when we finish shopping?"

"Of course."

"Is Layla going with us?"

"I'm going to check on her once I get dressed. I'm sure all she had was some sort of twenty-four-hour bug, though, and that she's fine."

"Good morning, Mommy," Layla said, walking into her sister's room and hugging her mom's waist. "Good morning, Jill."

"Well, I guess Jill and I talked you up, hunh? Good morning. Are you feeling better today?"

"A lot better. Are we going somewhere?"

Jillian and her mom laughed because Layla loved going anywhere, even if it was just down the street to the pharmacy.

"We're going to the grocery store and then maybe to run a couple of quick errands."

"Oh. Then are we leaving now?"

"First, you have to get some clothes on,"

their mother said, walking Layla out into the hallway and back toward her bedroom.

Jillian smiled at how cute her baby sister was and then went to her closet to see what she was going to wear today. After a few minutes, though, Layla came back into her sister's room and jumped onto her bed.

"I thought you were getting ready, little girl?"

"Jiiiill," she complained, the same as always. "I'm not a little girl."

Jillian smiled. "Oh yeah, that's right. I keep forgetting. You're a big girl."

"Is that what you're going to put on?" Layla asked, pointing at the hot-pink velour sweat suit Jillian was holding.

"Yep."

"That's pretty, and I'm going to tell Mom that I want to wear my pink sweat suit, too, so we can be dressed alike."

"Sounds good to me."

"So, did you have fun at the big dance last night?"

Jillian knew the "big dance" experience had been more like a nightmare than anything else, but she said, "Yeah, it was okay."

"Is there going to be another one?"

"In a couple of months or so maybe."

"Are you going?"

"Probably."

"Can I go with you?"

Jillian got a huge kick out of Layla and how she couldn't have cared less about asking the same questions over and over again, even if she'd already been told no before.

"Remember, the dances are only for the students who go to my school."

"Well, can I go somewhere else with you? Can I go with you the next time you go visit Nikki?"

"Well, not next time, which will be this afternoon, but maybe when I go over there another time. And then next weekend, we can go to the movies, if you want."

Layla hopped off the bed and hugged her sister. "I love you so much, Jill. You're the best sister in the whole wide world."

"I love you, too, Layla. You're the best sister in the whole wide world, too, and don't you ever forget that."

"I won't," she said, and then started out of the room when she heard their mother calling her.

Jillian gazed at Layla and then something dawned on her. It was true that her father was an awful man and that lately she'd been wishing and praying her mother had never met him, but the thing was, had he never become Jillian's stepfather — had he never married her mother — there would be no precious little Layla. Jillian would have no beautiful baby sister at all, and this she simply couldn't imagine. She couldn't imagine living one moment without the little girl who meant everything to her, and what a revelation that was. The kind of revelation that made Jillian's painful situation seem just a bit more bearable — the kind that encouraged her to keep her faith as strong as possible.

"Do you want to order a pizza or something?" Jillian asked Nikki.

"No."

Jillian had been sitting in Nikki's room for more than an hour, but in all that time, she hadn't done any more than answer Jillian's questions. Even then, she didn't elaborate and barely moved one inch. She was lying in her bed, turned on her left side, and was staring out her window.

"I'm so sorry that this happened to you," Jillian said for the umpteenth time. "And I wish I had stopped you from leaving with Marcus because maybe then you wouldn't have met those girls in the first place."

Jillian waited for a response. But there wasn't one.

"Nikki, please talk to me. I know you're sad and that you probably don't feel like being bothered by anyone, but I don't think it's good to keep all of this to yourself."

"You mean like when you kept your little problems to yourself not very long ago and cut me off like some stranger?"

Jillian knew she was right, but her feelings were still hurt. Nikki's words were so cold and unkind. "I'm sorry. And I'll leave if you want me to."

Jillian waited for her to say something and when she didn't, she grabbed her black leather purse and started toward the door.

"No, Jill, don't. I didn't mean it. Please don't leave."

Jillian dropped her bag back down and sat on the side of the bed Nikki was facing.

"This is just so hard for me to talk about is all. I can't believe anyone would hurt me like this. And for no reason, because I didn't do anything."

"I can't believe it either. It's so ridiculous, what they did to you."

"I would never treat anyone that way, so why would someone want to harm me?"

"I don't know. I wish I did, Nik, but I don't."

"I'll bet everyone at school will be talking about this for weeks. I'll be talked about and gawked at every day from now on."

"They'll probably talk about it for a while,

but no one will blame you for getting jumped by more than one person. Especially when you didn't even know those girls."

"I just don't understand why they would do it," she said, crying. "Three against one. It was so unfair."

Jillian rubbed her back, trying to comfort her, but had no words. She was speechless. Partly because she didn't know how many more times Nikki would want to hear her say how sorry she was, and partly because deep down she knew there was more to the story. There just had to be.

After a little time had passed, Nikki sat up and reached over for more tissues. "So, what's up with you and Kyle? With all this craziness, I never got to ask you. Did you guys have fun last night?"

"We did until the very end when my father saw us coming from around the side of the building."

Nikki squinted her eyes. "Why were you over there?"

"We didn't want anyone to see us kissing."

Nikki sniffled and then smiled for the first time since just before she'd left the dance with Marcus. "Really?"

"Yep."

"Wow. Kyle is a really nice boy, Jill, and

you're really lucky to have him. I know I said some nasty things about him yesterday, but I only said them because I didn't want to hear what you were saying."

"I like him, but now I can't even talk to him on the phone."

"Why?"

"When my father saw us, he got upset and started talking a bunch of stuff about Kyle wanting me to have sex with him. Which isn't even true, because Kyle already said he doesn't expect me to do anything I'm not ready for."

Nikki looked out of the window again, tears rolling down her face.

"Nik, what is it? Did I say something wrong?"

"No. It's those girls and what they did to me. No matter how hard I try, I just can't stop thinking about it."

"It'll get better, though. You'll see."

Nikki finally dropped off to sleep, and Jillian read the latest issue of *Glamour* magazine. It was around four in the afternoon, and she wondered if Kyle was home. She knew her father had basically forbidden her to have anything to do with him, but she really wanted to call him.

She debated a while longer and then

picked up Nikki's phone from the nightstand.

"Hello?"

"Hey, Kyle. It's me."

"Oh. When I saw the last name Gordon, I thought maybe it was for one of my parents."

"I'm at Nikki's."

"Really? How is she?"

"She's okay."

"That's good."

"So, have you been in all day?"

"My mom took me out to get some more athletic gear I needed, but that was it."

"Oh, okay."

"So, tell me something. Why did you get so upset when we kissed?"

Jillian had known he was probably going to ask her about that, but she'd been hoping it would be much later in the conversation and possibly on a whole other day.

"I guess I was kind of nervous, because I've never kissed a boy before."

"Yeah, but you acted like we were doing something bad and almost like I was hurting you."

"Well, I didn't mean to act that way, and I'm sorry."

"Maybe it'll be a lot better next time."

"It will."

"So, Nikki's really okay?" he said, changing the subject.

"Well, sort of, but she's sleeping now."

"Has she told you the truth yet about what happened?"

Jillian looked at Nikki, checking to see if she was in fact asleep, and said no.

"Well, I know the whole story."

"What story?"

"About Marcus and two of his friends from his neighborhood running a train on her. All three of them took turns doing it to her, and then they left her in the woods all by herself. And I also heard she was fine with it until Marcus started calling her all kinds of tramps and b's and told her he was through with her. And that's when she started crying and telling him she would do anything he wanted."

Kyle must have been mistaken. He was making this all up, and Jillian didn't know why. "Who told you that?"

"One of my boys called me this morning. The whole team knows about it, because Marcus has already been bragging the same as usual."

"I don't believe that. Marcus is no good, but this is even too low-down for him. I just don't think he would go that far."

"He would, and he did. Trust me."

Nikki turned and looked at Jillian. "Kyle, I have to go."

"Who was that?" Nikki asked when Jillian hung up.

"Kyle."

"And why were you talking about Marcus?"

"Because he was saying that Marcus and two other guys ran a train on you, and that Marcus also called you all kinds of names."

Nikki frowned. "That's insane. And your little boyfriend had better stop spreading all those lies about me."

"He's not. He was just repeating what he heard."

"Well, it's not true."

"Then why would people be saying it?"

"I don't know, but Marcus would never make me do anything like that."

"Okay, then, what really happened?"

"Marcus and I went up in the woods just like I told you, and it was just the two of us."

"Well, if you were with just Marcus the whole time, then where was he when those girls jumped you?"

"I'm not talking about this anymore."

Jillian watched Nikki turn back toward the window and knew Kyle wasn't lying. Marcus and his boys had treated Nikki no different from the prostitutes she'd seen standing on corners on the southeast side of town, and now Nikki was embarrassed about it. She was humiliated in the worst way.

"Nik, did they force you? Because if they did, then that means they raped you and you should tell your mom. You have to tell her so that the police can arrest them."

"Didn't you hear me?" she yelled, now looking at Jillian. "Didn't you hear me when I said it never happened? And if you're really my friend, you'll stop listening to Kyle or anyone else, and you'll only listen to me. You'll believe what I've been telling you since last night. Okay?"

Jillian finally relented and agreed to what Nikki was asking. She went along with what she wanted but wondered if Nikki would eventually have to confess . . . or be like her and never tell another living soul.

CHAPTER 14

Monday, October 27, 2008

I just arrived home from school and thankfully, Daddy isn't home yet. All weekend, I caught him looking at me in his usual eerie way, and what I keep hoping is that he won't start messing with me again. I've been thinking about that a lot over the last couple of days, and I also can't stop thinking about Kyle and the really rude way I treated him Friday evening. I don't know why I pushed him away or why when he'd been kissing me, I kept seeing Daddy's face. I also don't know why I felt so dirty. The good news is that Kyle isn't angry with me about it, but I do wonder if the same thing will happen the next time we're together again and all alone.

Jillian set her pen on her desk and looked at the photo of her and Nikki, sitting atop her dresser. Nikki hadn't come to school today, but everyone had still gone on and on about what had happened. Word had traveled around the school in nothing flat, and Jillian could only imagine how hard it was going to be for Nikki once she returned. Especially if a lot of their schoolmates continued saying such harsh things about her. They'd called her every deplorable name they could think of, even worse than the words Marcus had supposedly called Nikki, and Jillian knew Nikki would never be able to take it. At one point, a couple of boys had even asked Jillian how she could still be friends with such a loose little whore, but Jillian had tried her best to ignore them. Later, she'd even seen one of them giving Marcus a high five, like what he'd done to Nikki was something to be proud of. Then Ashley and Shelly, her and Nikki's so-called close friends, had made their own not-so-nice comments, too, which Jillian was very shocked about, and it was the reason she'd kept to herself most of the day. She'd even gone to the library instead of going to lunch, and if things weren't any better tomorrow, she would dodge the cafeteria all over again.

Jillian reached for the phone and dialed Nikki's number, but when she didn't get an answer, she picked up her pen and wrote a few more lines in her journal. At first, she wrote a bit more about her trying day at school, but then she focused on the deranged way her father had acted right after the dance. Specifically, when they'd left Nikki's and were on their way home.

I had never seen him so angry and had never witnessed him driving so fast, and I was terrified the whole time. He'd acted no differently than some of the disturbed criminals I sometimes see on TV, but even stranger was how calm and normal he became when we walked in the house and saw Mom. It had almost been like watching two totally different people, which was very bizarre.

She wrote for a while longer but soon heard a door close downstairs. She knew it could easily be her mother, but something told her it was her father instead. Sadly, she was right, and soon he was standing directly in front of her.

"I just wanna talk is all."

Jillian kept quiet.

"I've really missed our special times, and you really hurt me a few weeks ago when you kept saying you were going to tell your mother everything. I felt so betrayed, be-

cause no one, not your mom or your grandparents, loves you as much as I do, yet
you've been trying so hard to turn against
me. I know you're still not all that comfortable with what you and I have together, but
believe me when I say we've never done
anything wrong."

"I just don't like it when we do those
things, Daddy. I don't like it, and all I want
is for us to be like any other regular father
and daughter. I want us to be normal like
everyone else."

"But that's what I've always tried to get
you to see. Our relationship *is* normal. We
don't just say we love each other like a lot
of parents and children do, we genuinely
show it. And that means so much more than
you realize."

"I don't realize it because if it's okay for
us to be doing this kind of stuff, then why
don't you want Mom to know? Why don't
you want me telling anybody?"

"Because, princess, they won't understand, and if you tell them it will ruin
everything. I've tried explaining this to you
for years, so why can't you just trust me?
Why can't you just enjoy what we have and
forget about everyone else?"

"I still don't understand, and whenever
we did those things, I always felt so

ashamed."

His tone changed. "Oh yeah? Well, did you also feel *ashamed* when you were kissing that little punk?"

Jillian peered at the floor, but her father placed his hand under her chin and raised her head back up. "Princess, look, I know you're at the age where all kinds of little boys are going to start coming after you, but they'll never be able to give you what I can. They'll never be able to do what a real man is capable of doing. And while I'm a little embarrassed to tell you this, when I saw you with that boy, Kyle, I almost got sick at the stomach. I was so jealous and so hurt."

Now Jillian knew for sure that her father had lost his mind. He must have with the way he was talking to her right now.

"Princess, I don't just want you, I need you. I need you real bad, and I wanna show you."

"No. I won't start back doing all those awful things. I won't, Daddy." The last time she'd told him no and that she was telling, he'd left her alone for weeks, and she hoped her saying no was going to work again.

"Even after all I do for you? I mean, look at this bedroom of yours and all those clothes in your closet. Do you think you'd have any of this if it was still just you and your mom?"

"I won't do it. I just won't."

"You're really starting to hurt my feelings again, and I wish you wouldn't do that. I wish you'd stop before I have to do some things I would rather not do."

Jillian stared at him.

"But if you force me, I'm going to tell your mother what I saw you doing to that boy when I came to pick you up. Remember what I told you on Friday night? That I'll have no choice but to tell her about that blow job you were giving him. And don't forget I still have all those nice photos I took of you, and if you force me, I'll do more than show them to your mom. I'll print lots of copies and make sure they get passed around at your school. I don't want to do it, but I'm willing to do whatever I have to in order to be with you. I love you, princess, and if you'll only give me a chance, I'll show you that you don't need some little boy like Kyle. Which the more I think about it, I think he's the real reason you've all of a sudden lost interest in me."

"Daddy, I have homework to do, and Mom will be home really soon."

"Fine. But don't say I didn't try my best to make things right with you when I move on to someone else. Don't say I didn't give you a chance when I start spending special time with little Layla. My precious baby girl is only five, but we all know how smart she is for her age. She'll learn just as quickly as you did when you were seven."

Jillian's eyes widened. "Daddy, no. Please don't."

"I don't want to, and I never have until this day. But fathers have their needs. They have needs that have to be fulfilled and if one daughter won't do it, I'll have no choice but to teach another one how to."

Jillian had known this day was going to come. She'd figured it out weeks ago, and it was the reason she'd stopped thinking about the idea of taking her own life. The thought had still entered her mind every now and then, but not so much once she'd started praying and asking God to remove it.

But living or dying was neither here nor there, because she could never let him touch Layla. She *wouldn't* let him. Instead, she would do, strongly against her will, what she had to.

"Okay. I'll do whatever you want, Daddy, but please leave Layla alone. Please don't mess with her."

Her father smiled. "That's my girl," he said, sliding his belt open. "That's my sweet little princess."

Jillian braced herself all while watching his pants and underwear dropping to the floor. They dropped, and this time, he never even bothered closing her blinds.

CHAPTER 15

In the past, her father had always made sure the lighting in her room was pretty dim, so Jillian had never gotten a real good look at her father's thing before. Now that she had, she despised what they were doing even more. She hated this. Still, though, after he had released himself in her mouth and walked out of her room, she had reconfirmed in her mind that it was her responsibility to protect Layla and that she would do whatever her father asked from now on. She would take care of him whenever he wanted her to, and she told herself that at least he wasn't making her have intercourse. Giving him oral sex was the worst, but it still couldn't be nearly as bad as going all the way, not to mention she didn't even have to spend time with him every single day.

Jillian finished the last of her homework and tried calling Nikki again. This time she picked up.

"Hey, Jill."

"Hey. How are you?"

"I'm okay, I guess."

"I called you when I first got home from school, but you didn't answer."

"My mom ran to the store, and I never even looked to see who was calling."

"Are you coming to school tomorrow?"

"I don't know yet. Maybe."

"If not, I'll come by tomorrow after key club to hang out with you for a little while if you want."

Nikki paused and then said, "So was it real bad?"

"Was what bad?"

"All the gossip and all the rumors. I mean, was everyone saying nasty things about me?"

This was the last question Jillian wanted to answer truthfully, but she did. "You know how some of those kids are. They talk about everybody no matter what's going on."

"Did you see Marcus?"

"Yeah, once. But that was it."

"Did he ask about me?"

"No. He didn't."

Nikki sniffled multiple times, and Jillian knew she was crying.

"I just don't understand what I did wrong. I don't understand why he won't talk to me.

I did everything he asked me to do, and now he's acting like he can't even stand me. I even called him last night but when his mom called him to the phone, all he did was hang up on me. He never said one word."

"I don't understand either. I don't get Marcus at all. But, Nik, you deserve a lot better than the way he's doing you. There are so many other boys that like you, so forget Marcus."

"But I love him, Jill. I love him so much."

Jillian was lost for words.

"He told me that if I did this one thing for him, I would be his girl from now on. He told me that if I did what he wanted, he would never even look at another girl again. He made me so many promises."

Jillian debated whether she should ask Nikki what it was he'd wanted her to do, but she couldn't help herself. "What did he ask you to do?"

Nikki broke into tears again but soon settled down.

"You already know because Kyle told you on Saturday. Marcus asked me to do it with him and two of his friends, and I did. I did it with all three of them, and now he won't even speak to me."

Jillian sighed. "I can't stand Marcus. I

never liked him, not even a little."

"I just don't get why he's doing this, because I even let him do it to me without a condom. He didn't use one the first time we did it, and he didn't use one on Friday night either. His two friends did, but Marcus said that since I was his girl, he needed to feel all of me with nothing in between and that we didn't need any protection."

"Oh my God, Nik. You don't think you're pregnant, do you?"

"I don't know. I'm so scared because if I am, my mom is going to kill me."

"This is horrible."

Nikki cried out loud again, and Jillian sat holding the phone. Maybe this whole conversation was nothing more than some wicked dream Jillian would soon wake up from.

But she knew this was only wishful thinking. She knew she was sitting there on the phone with her best friend and that what she'd just confessed was reality. What had happened to Nikki was real, and there was no taking it back. No chance to rethink anything, no chance to reconsider, no chance to reevaluate. The damage had already been done and now all she could do was deal with the consequences.

"Jill, what am I going to do?"

"I'm going to start praying right now that you're not pregnant, and you need to do the same thing."

"I will, but what if prayer doesn't work?"

"We have to believe that it will."

"How could I be so stupid?"

"Don't say that, Nik."

"But I am. I was so stupid for doing those things for Marcus and then thinking he really loved me. I was stupid for not listening to you."

"We all make mistakes, and my mom always says that there's nothing wrong with that as long as you learn something from it."

"Speaking of moms," Nikki hurried to say. "I hear mine calling me and she sounds upset. I'd better call you back."

"Talk to you later."

Jillian ended the call but when she thought she heard loud voices, she turned her television down. She listened, and it sounded like her parents were arguing. Jillian knew she was probably wrong about that, though, because her parents barely even disagreed about anything and she could only remember a couple of times in all the years they'd been together that they'd even been angry with each other. Even then, they'd barely raised their voices, and it was never long before she saw them hugging and smiling again.

But when Jillian eased open her door and heard her mother say, "Byron, please tell me you haven't been sleeping with another woman," her heart skipped a beat.

"Baby, of course I haven't," he insisted. "You know I would never do anything like that. This is just some childish eighteen-year-old girl, right out of high school, who's got some silly little crush on me. That's all this is about, and she's lying through her teeth."

"Well, if that's true, then why is she saying that the two of you get a hotel room every Wednesday during your lunch hour, when *you're* supposed to be out doing claim reviews? And if she's lying, why would she give me her phone number?"

"I don't know why. Maybe she's crazy."

"But, Byron, she even says that you've been sleeping together ever since she was hired at your company four months ago."

"I don't care what she says. She's lying."

"Does she work in your department?"

"No, she works in the switchboard room, and unless she transfers a call to me, I never even talk to her."

For a few seconds, neither of them said anything, but Jillian didn't move. Then her father finally spoke again.

"Look, honey, I'm really sorry that this has happened and that you're so upset, but I promise you on my life that I've never touched this girl. I've never even considered it, and if you think about it, what on earth would I want with a child? Why would I have anything to do with someone that much younger than me?"

"I just don't understand why she would lie about something like this."

"I already told you. She probably has some sort of crush on me, but I'm sure it'll pass in no time."

"I want to talk to her."

"For what?!" he yelled.

"Because I do. And I'm going to."

"You mean to tell me you're going to believe some fickle teenage girl over your own husband?"

"I never said that. But at the same time, there's no way I can just simply ignore all the stuff in this letter. I mean, would you?"

"Of course I would. I would ignore it because I trust you. I trust you with everything in me, and no one could ever make me feel any differently."

"That's very easy for you to say, though, because I've never given you the slightest reason to feel otherwise. Not ever."

"And neither have I. I mean, baby, come on. This is me. The man who loves you and who has always loved you. The man who would never even think of touching another woman, let alone some girl."

Jillian raised her eyebrows, begging to differ with his last statement.

"But that's just it, Byron," her mother said. "She's not just some *girl*. Legally, she's a grown woman. A grown woman who is obviously tired of sharing you with your wife."

"I really don't believe you, Roxanne. I mean, not after all the years we've been together and how wonderful of a husband I've always tried to be to you. Not after all the years I've tried to be a perfect father to our girls."

"I know that, and I want to believe that this woman is lying, but I need peace with all of this. I need peace of mind, and the only way I'll be able to get that is by talking with her."

"And what if this gets out at my job? I mean, what if she tells other people that you confronted her? Then what?"

Jillian's mother didn't respond.

"Roxanne, baby, please, don't do this."

"Look, Byron, I love you with all my heart, but if I don't find out the truth, things will never be the same between us. I'll always be suspicious of everything you do, and I could never live like that. Even now, I've got a ton of terrible thoughts going through my head, and my heart is literally aching."

"But —"

"My mind is made up. I'm calling this Deanna woman now, and if she can't prove any of what's in this letter, then I'll never bring it up again."

"Baby, please wait."

"Wait for what?"

"Oh God, what have I done?" Jillian heard her father say.

"Byron, what are you talking about?"

"Baby, please sit down so I can talk to you."

"No! Just tell me."

"Okay, okay. Honey, I did something really stupid. Something so far outside of my character that even I can't figure it out."

"What?"

"Roxie, this will be so much easier if you'll just sit down."

"No. Now, just tell me."

"Okay . . . it's true. I did sleep with her, but last week I told her it was over."

"You what?!"

"I'm so sorry, baby, but I swear it will

never happen again. Not for as long as I live."

"Don't touch me," Jillian heard her mother say. "Don't you dare come near me."

"But, baby —"

"Byron, I want you out of here."

"All because of one mistake?"

"You heard me."

"Look, baby, I know you're upset and that I've hurt you really bad, but please, let's talk about this."

"I need to be alone."

"Baby, please don't shut me out. Please let me explain what happened."

"Get out of here, Byron!"

"Mommy, Daddy, why are you yelling at each other?" Jillian heard Layla say, and went to make sure her sister was okay.

"Layla, sweetie, everything is fine," her mother said. "Mommy and Daddy are just talking."

"Mom, what's wrong?" Jillian asked when she walked into their room, even though she'd heard every word.

"Honey, please take your sister into your room and close the door behind you."

"Come on, Layla," she said, grabbing her hand and escorting her down the hallway.

"Jill, why is Mommy crying?"

"I don't know."

Layla burst into tears, and Jillian sat down on her bed. "Come here," she told her. "Don't worry. Everything'll be fine just like Mom said."

Jillian tried reassuring her, but to be honest, she wasn't sure how things were actually going to play out. There was no way to know one way or the other, but she hoped her prayers were about to be answered. She hoped her father really was moving out — for good.

CHAPTER 16

Jillian and Layla walked into the kitchen and sat across from each other. "Good morning, Mom," "Good morning, Mommy," they each said one after the other.

"Good morning, girls," she responded, and Jillian saw tears forming in her mother's eyes. "Breakfast is almost ready."

Jillian hated seeing her so upset, and just knowing that her father was the cause of it made it all that much worse. Ironically, he was now entering from the garage, looking as though he was some sort of victim. He wore a noticeably pitiful expression on his face, but Jillian wasn't buying it.

He sat down at the table with them. "There's something I need to talk to you girls about. I've thought about how I would tell you this, but the truth of the matter is there's no easy way to say this, except, Daddy's going to have to go away for a while."

Layla wrinkled her forehead. "Why,

Daddy?"

"It's sort of hard to explain, but Daddy and Mommy need to spend a little time apart."

"Is that why Mommy was crying last night?"

"Yes. Daddy made a mistake, but he's very sorry about it."

"What kind of a mistake?"

Jillian couldn't wait to hear his response.

"It was a grown folks kind of mistake, but what I can tell you is that I'll never make a mistake like this again and that I know for sure that God is going to work everything out. I love Mommy, and I love you and Jill, and I promise I'll make things right and will be back home in no time."

Layla looked at him, then at her mom, and then at Jillian with misty eyes. "Daddy, I don't want you to leave us."

Their father reached his hands out to her, and she went over and climbed onto his lap.

"Pumpkin, I know this is hard for you, but everything really will be all right," he said, and then looked at Jillian. "I know this is painful for you too, princess. It's painful for all of us."

Was he serious? Did he honestly think she was feeling even the slightest bit of grief about his leaving? If he did, he was crazy. If he had any sense at all, he'd know just how overjoyed she was and that she couldn't have been happier.

Her father hugged Layla for a few seconds and kissed her on her forehead. Then he stood, stepped around the table, and did the same thing to Jillian, who still said not one word to him.

After that, he walked over to their mother. "Baby, please. I'm begging you to reconsider. It'll be so much easier for us to try to work things out if I'm right here with you."

"Byron, please just go."

Jillian watched him pause for a few seconds, displaying a pathetic and sad look on his face, but then he finally grabbed his duffel bag and left. She was sure he needed a lot more clothing than that, so maybe he'd already packed the rest of his things in his truck. What she hoped was that he'd taken just about everything he owned, so he wouldn't have to come back there any time soon.

Their mother wiped the wetness from her face and then set a bowl of grits, a dish of scrambled eggs, and a plate of turkey sausage links down in front of them. Sadly, though, Layla cried more intensely and their mother tried consoling her. Jillian hated seeing her baby sister so unhappy, and she felt even worse for her mom, who was now shedding just as many tears herself. She felt terrible and even a little guilty because for her, today was a wonderful time of celebration.

Her mother sniffled a couple of times and then looked up. "Jill, I know this is just as difficult for you as it is for Layla, and I'm so sorry that we have to go through this."

"No, Mom. I'm the one who feels sorry."

"Sorry for what, sweetie? You didn't do anything."

"I'm sorry that you're feeling so sad."

"I know, but I'll be fine. We'll all be fine. You'll see."

Her mother sat holding Layla for a few minutes longer until she was much calmer, and then Jillian and Layla ate their food. They mostly sat in silence, and when they finished, Layla went back up to her room to watch television, something she always did whenever it wasn't quite time for her to leave for school yet.

Their mother opened the dishwasher and stacked inside one dish and utensil after another. "So, how's Nikki doing?"

"When I spoke to her last night, she was still feeling kind of down, and she didn't sound much better when she called here this morning."

"Is she going to school today?"

"Uh-huh. Her mom is driving her, though, and she wanted to know if I would ride with them," she said, but didn't tell her that Miss G had found out the truth and was actually *demanding* that Nikki go back to school today.

"Well, unfortunately, it's probably going to be very hard for her, because I got a call from Shelly's mom yesterday saying that some little boy Nikki was calling herself going with talked her into having sex with him and two of his friends."

Jillian was shocked to hear what her mother had just said because she hadn't planned on telling her mother anything. Not about the kids at school and all the rumors they were spreading or that, yesterday, Nikki had finally admitted the truth to her.

"So, is that what happened?" her mother asked.

"Mom, Nikki is my friend, and I don't want to say anything that will get her into trouble."

"That's all well and good, but I can't help worrying about the effect all this is having on you. Don't get me wrong. You've always been the model child, and I've always been very happy about that, but it's like I'm always telling you, I still remember what it was like being twelve. You become a lot more interested in boys, and sex is always an issue."

"But I'm not like Nikki, and I would never let any boy talk me into doing that kind of stuff."

"Well, I'm really glad to hear that, because at your age, sex should be the furthest thing from your mind. You, Nikki, and every other girl should be focusing on school and on having the kind of fun young ladies can be proud of. Sex is something you shouldn't even have to think about until you're a whole lot older."

Jillian slightly changed the subject. "I just feel bad for Nikki because I know all those kids at school are going to be so mean to her."

"I feel bad for her, too, and also for her mom, because I'm sure this has got to be one of the toughest and most embarrassing incidents they've ever experienced."

Jillian agreed with her mom and glanced over at the clock on the microwave. She knew Nikki and Miss G would be there any moment, so she stood up, grabbed her book bag from the corner of her chair, and slid it over her shoulder. But when she saw her mother crying again, she dropped her bag back down and went over to her. "Mom, what's wrong?"

"Oh, nothing, sweetie. I'm okay, and you'd better get going."

"But I can miss school today if you want. I can stay home if you need me to."

"Honey, no. I'm just a little upset about your father and me, and I miss him already."

Her mother's words forced an ice-cold chill up Jillian's spine. "Well, at least you still have Layla and me."

"I know. And don't you worry about a thing, because I'm already praying for God to fix this. I'm praying that your father and I will be able to get past these problems we're having, so that the four of us can get back to being just as happy as always."

Jillian hugged her mother good-bye but didn't dare say what she was thinking — that *she* was praying, too — except her prayer was for a totally different outcome. She didn't have it in her heart to tell her mom that what she really wanted was for her to file for a divorce.

Just as Jillian prepared to head toward the front door, Layla came back into the kitchen. "Mommy, when are we leaving?"

"In about ten minutes, so why don't you run upstairs and grab my purse?"

"You're going to work in a T-shirt and sweat pants?"

"No, Mommy isn't going to work today. She's staying home to get some rest."

"Oh."

Layla ran back upstairs again, and Jillian heard Miss G honking her horn. "See ya later, Lay," she yelled up to her sister, and then hugged her mother a second time. "I love you, Mom."

"I love you, too, sweetie, and you have a good day."

CHAPTER 17

When Miss G pulled in front of the school, the bell still hadn't rung yet and all nine-hundred-plus pairs of eyes settled on Nikki.

"Oh my God, Mom, look at them. Look how hard they're staring over here."

"And?" Miss G said angrily. Jillian had never seen her so furious.

"Mom, I can't do this. I just can't. So, please let me go back home for at least another day."

"You should have thought about that when you were spreading your legs for those mannish little boys."

Jillian didn't move an inch. She was afraid to even blink.

Nikki turned all the way toward her mother. "I'm so sorry, Mom, but please don't make me go in there."

"Like I said, you should have thought about all of this before you did something so stupid. And don't get me started on that ridiculous lie you made up about those mysterious girls jumping you. You lied straight to my face, and now you're going to have to deal with the consequences. Then, when school is out, I want you to bring your little sneaky behind straight back home because it's like I told you this morning, you're grounded for the next three months. No TV, no iPod, and unless it's about homework, no phone calls, no computer, and no company. And I'm still calling that boy's parents when we get home this evening."

Nikki eased open the car door and stepped out, and Jillian, fearfully, thanked Miss G for the ride.

As they strode through the crowd of students and up closer to the building, tons of them pointed and whispered and some even sniggled. Nikki looked back at her mom, who was driving away, and Jillian said, "Forget these silly kids, Nik. Don't even think about them." Words that were all great advice until they walked inside and a clique of girls that included Ashley and Shelly gawked at Nikki like she had some sort of contagious disease.

"Choooo-choooo, choooo-choooo," one of them vocalized, mimicking the sound of a train.

Jillian nudged Nikki along. "Girl, just ignore them."

But as they continued through the hallway to Nikki's locker, these same girls, at least seven of them, followed closely behind.

"Just look at that little tramp," the tall, stout one said; she was obviously the ringleader. "Lettin' three boys run a train on her like some low-life hooker."

Nikki looked at Jillian, and all seven girls laughed out loud. Jillian was astonished at how quickly Ashley and Shelly had turned on Nikki. They were such traitors, and Jillian was done being friends with them.

The ringleader moved closer to Nikki. "That's what that little trick gets for tryin' to be all that. Thinkin' she's so cute."

They stood for a few seconds longer and then walked away, still ranting one awful thing after another. When they were out of sight, Nikki dialed in her combination, opened her locker, hung up her leather jacket and backpack, and pulled out her history book. When she closed it, she and Jillian turned around to more bad news: Marcus and his teammates. Jillian could tell Nikki was practically praying that Marcus would say something to her — anything — but all he did was glare at her with a smirk, shake his head like she was nothing, and keep going. His friends snickered like she was a huge joke, and soon after, Jillian saw tears rolling down Nikki's face again.

"Don't worry about them," Jillian told her. "I'll walk with you to your first class and if you need me, all you have to do is come get me out of mine."

"I have to take this letter my mom wrote to the office. It's for my absence yesterday."

"Is she planning to report what happened on Friday to the principal?"

"I think she is, and if she does, Jill, Marcus will never speak to me again. He'll never have anything else to do with me."

It was probably better for Jillian not to comment one way or the other, because if she did, she was sure Nikki wouldn't be too happy with her — not when, right now, all Jillian could think about was how naïve and simple Nikki was acting. How lovesick she was over Marcus when even little Layla would have the sense enough to see that Marcus wanted nothing to do with her. He'd used her for sex and sex only, and the sooner Nikki realized that, the better off she would be.

Only seconds after the bell rang, Jillian walked out of fourth period and saw Kyle standing and waiting for her.

"So, how was class?" he asked as they started down the hallway.

"Good."

"Do you have to go to your locker?"

"Yeah, I need to drop off my books."

"It's really too bad we can't talk on the phone. You know that, don't you?"

"What if I call you tonight?"

"That's cool with me, but what about your dad?"

"Well, it's not like he pays that much attention to every call I make, anyway, so I'll just make sure I call you when he's not around."

"As long as you won't get into trouble."

"I won't."

When they arrived at Jillian's locker, Nikki looked sadder than she had this morning. "I'm not going into that cafeteria," she said matter-of-factly.

Jillian turned toward Kyle. "Hey, I'll have to see you later, okay?"

"No problem. I'll talk to you tonight," he said, and left.

Nikki tried her best to smile. "Thanks, Jill. Thanks for sticking by my side and not cutting me off the way Ashley and Shelly have."

"Girl, please. I would never do that to you. You're my best friend, and you'll always be able to count on me. Let's just go into the library."

"Okay," Nikki agreed, but before they could take the first step in that direction, Marcus and four of his boys walked in front of them.

"So, what were you saying about that Nikki chick, Marcus?" the ugly one asked, acting as if Nikki wasn't even standing there.

"What?"

"You know. The part about her being the dumbest girl you've ever been with."

"Oh yeah. I guess I did say that, didn't I? Shoot, I've got so many young hos runnin' behind me till I can barely keep 'em straight."

They all cracked up like they were watching a comedy show.

"I heard that, Marcus, man," the ugly one continued. "Use those hos and then leave 'em right where you found 'em."

Marcus looked at Nikki, but she and Jillian kept walking. His posse laughed even louder.

"Marcus, why are you doing this?" Nikki finally said. "Why are you being so cruel when just last week you said you loved me?"

Marcus stopped in his tracks.

"Girl, you must be crazy. I could never love you. I could never love any girl who gives it up faster than I can ask for it and then has no problem being with as many other guys as I tell her to."

Nikki was speechless.

Marcus shook his head in disgust and then one of the other boys said, "Plus, Marcus, man, I can't believe that skank thought she had you so fooled."

"I know. Had me thinkin' she was some innocent little virgin when she knew good and well she was just as broken in as all the rest of these freaks around here. That chick was wide open, and if I didn't know any better, I'd swear she'd already been with a full-grown man."

They laughed again and went on their way.

Jillian was thunderstruck.

"Oh my God, Jill," Nikki hurried to say, but she seemed nervous and couldn't keep eye contact with Jillian for longer than a couple of seconds. "Marcus has everyone thinking the absolute worst of me. They think I'm the biggest tramp in school, and there's no way I can stay here. I have to go home."

Jillian desperately wanted to ask her about the not-being-a-virgin thing but didn't. "How will you get there?"

"I don't know. Because you saw how angry my mom was. She's totally through, and she'll never leave work to come get me."

"What about your dad?"

"He's working, too."

Jillian thought about her own mother and how she hadn't gone to work today. If Jillian called and explained how bad things were for Nikki there at school, she knew her mom would gladly come pick her up. The only thing was, Jillian didn't want anyone knowing about her parents and the problems they were having, and it was the reason she hadn't uttered one word to Nikki. Of course, it was true that Jillian was more than thrilled about her father's moving out, but what she didn't want was people finding out that he'd cheated on her mother with an eighteen-year-old. The whole idea of it was beyond humiliating, and she didn't want to be ridiculed.

But none of that mattered right now, because Nikki was more important. She needed her help, and Jillian would do whatever she could to give it to her. Which was why she pulled her cell phone from her shoulder purse, the one she pretty much only used for texting and emergency phone calls. Although, in all honesty, she didn't text nearly as often as most kids her age.

"My mom took the day off, so maybe we can call her."

"Do you think she'll be mad?"

"No, not at all," Jillian said, dialing the number, and her mother answered almost immediately.

"Hi, sweetie."

"Hi, Mom."

"Is everything okay?"

"No, not really. Things are pretty bad for Nikki, and she wants to go home."

"Did she call her mom?"

"No, because she's at work."

"Well, I don't mind coming to get her, but I won't do it unless her mom says it's okay."

"I'll have Nikki call her now and then I'll call you back."

When Jillian pressed the end button, Nikki said, "I'm too afraid, Jill, so can you please do it for me?"

Jillian felt the same but went ahead and made the call. "Miss G? This is Jillian."

"What's wrong with Nikki?" she said without hesitation.

"Nothing . . . well . . . actually Nikki is having a really hard time being here. And, Miss G, it's really bad. Those boys are saying such ugly things about her and a lot of the girls are, too. They're saying stuff after every single class, and since my mom is off today, she said she didn't mind coming to get Nikki if you said it was okay."

"Fine, but you tell her that she'd better go home with your mom and stay there until I pick her up this evening. I don't want her even thinking about going home by herself because she's already proven that she can't be trusted."

"Do you want to speak to her?"

"No, because I don't have one thing to say to that girl."

"Thanks, Miss G."

"Good-bye."

Jillian escorted Nikki to the school office the same as she had that morning and told her she'd see her when she got home. Then she headed toward her next class, which she had a test in. She felt sorry for Nikki, but she couldn't wait to ask her the most important question of all: who *else* she'd had sex with but hadn't bothered telling her about.

CHAPTER 18

Jillian stepped away from the bus and onto the sidewalk and waved good-bye to a girl in her math class. She lived only three blocks from where she was standing, and she couldn't wait to get home to see how Nikki was doing.

But as she strolled closer and closer to her house, suddenly her heart beat wildly and her stomach twirled briskly. Her father's SUV was sitting in the driveway, and already she had a bad feeling about it. Although, maybe he'd simply dropped by to pick up Layla for a little while or maybe pick up more of his belongings.

Jillian walked a few more feet into the driveway and into the garage, which was open, and went inside. She looked around but when she didn't see or hear anyone down on the first floor, she went upstairs and saw that her parents' bedroom door was shut. This made her even more nervous, so she went into her own room, thinking Nikki would be there waiting. But she wasn't.

Next, Jillian went into Layla's room as well, but she wasn't anywhere to be found either. However, as soon as she headed back toward her own room, her mother opened the door to hers and walked out into the hallway with a robe on. Jillian wasn't sure what to say, but she knew what her mother and father had probably been in there doing. Especially since her mother had closed their bedroom door right behind her and her hair was scattered out of place.

"Oh, hi, sweetie," she said, acting as though she was a bit self-conscious. "I thought I heard someone come up the stairs, but I didn't know you'd made it home already. How was your day?"

"It was okay. But where's Nikki?"

"Well, when I first picked her up, she seemed fine, but as we drove away from the school, she started crying and wouldn't tell me what was wrong. So, I called her mother, and she ended up having to leave work after all to come get her."

"How long was she here?"

"Maybe an hour at the most."

"Where's Layla?"

"I asked Mom to pick her up for me so that your dad and I could have some time to talk. He left work early today."

"Oh," Jillian responded, and then started back toward her room.

"Jill, honey, wait. Remember when I said to you this morning that everything was going to be fine?"

"Yes."

"Well, it really is. Your father and I still have to work some things out, but we decided that we can't do that if we're separated. Plus, it wouldn't be fair to you and Layla if we split up without even trying to fix this problem we're having. Your dad made a mistake, but he's very sorry about it."

What Jillian wanted to tell her was that she'd heard their whole conversation last night and that she knew his so-called *mistake* had been his having sex with an eighteen-year-old. She wanted to tell her that he'd done everything but go all the way with her, too — her own twelve-year-old daughter. But she didn't.

"Are you hungry?" her mother asked.

"No."

"Well, I'll be going down to cook something in a little while."

"I have homework to do anyway."

"Okay, then you go ahead, and I'll let you know when dinner is ready."

Jillian was heartbroken. How could her mom be so okay with what her father had done to her? With what he'd done to their marriage? And why was she acting as if his having an affair wasn't all that bad? Jillian couldn't believe her mother had allowed him to come back so quickly and that she even had a peaceful smile on her face. As a matter of fact, she seemed almost relieved about the entire situation.

Jillian plopped down on her bed and felt even more trapped than she had in the past, because if her father could outright admit that he'd been having sex with a teenager and then sway her mom back into bed with him less than twenty-four hours later, there was surely no hope of her mother ever believing Jillian over her father. She realized, once again, that her father continued to be right about her mother and how if Jillian ever told her mother anything, it would be her word against his and that her mother would always side with him.

Jillian walked into her closet, removed five shoe boxes stacked on top of one another, and pulled her journal from a sixth one. Then, after replacing the boxes back, she went over to her bed, turned on her television, and wrote the first words.

Tuesday, October 28, 2008

Why can't Mom see Daddy for who he really is? And how could she take him back so quickly? How could she ever trust him again about anything? And why doesn't it matter to her that this girl, woman, or whatever you want to call her, is young enough to be his daughter? I mean, Daddy is five years older than Mom and that means he's twenty years older than this Deanna person. It just doesn't make any sense, and I just wish Mom would somehow figure out how slick and phony Daddy actually is. I just wish there was some way she could find out the truth about him. I wish there was a way I could tell her and know for sure she would believe me. I wish I could just be free. I remember when I was about four years old and Great-grandmother Cecile used to say, "If I had wings, I'd fly away and be at rest," and now I know what she meant. She was so tired of being sick all the time and doing so much suffering, and I'm starting to get just as tired as she was.

Jillian wrote a while longer and then thought about Nikki. She so wanted to call and check on her but now that Nikki was on punishment, she doubted that Miss G would let her talk to her. So, she decided to sign on to AOL to see if maybe Nikki had by chance snuck online, and thankfully she had. Jillian smiled and clicked her mouse inside the narrow box to the right, and an instant message window opened. Jillian's screen name was Jillian22, and while both she and Nikki had signed up on the same day and had planned all along to choose screen names as close to the same as possible, neither of them had any idea what was so special about the number 22, but since Nikki had insisted on how cool it sounded, they'd gone with it.

Jillian22: Hey, Nik. How are you? Mom said you were really upset this afternoon.

Nikki22: I was but I'm okay now.

Jillian22: What was wrong?

Nikki22: I couldn't stop thinking about Marcus and how mean he was to me. And then I kept thinking about what everyone else was saying too.

Jillian22: They're all wrong for acting this way and I hate that they're doing this to you.

Nikki22: I don't want to go back there. But my mom says that I made my own bed and now I have to lie in it. She's so mad at me.

Jillian22: I could tell this morning.

Nikki22: Jill, what am I going to do?

Jillian22: I don't know.

Nikki22: I'm so embarrassed about everything.

Jillian wondered if this was a good time to ask her about those terrible things Marcus had said about her today, the part about her being broken in and wide open. More than anything, she still wondered why Nikki hadn't told her about being with some other boy.

Nikki22: Hey, I have to go.

Jillian22: OK. And, Nik, things will be better tomorrow. You'll see.

Nikki22: I hope so.

Jillian browsed through some of the headline news stories AOL had posted and then picked up the phone and called her grandparents and Layla.

"Hello?"

"Hi, Grandma, how are you?"

"I'm fine, Jill. How are you?"

"I'm good. And how is Grandpa?"

"He's doing well, too, and Miss Layla has him in the den watching some show on Disney."

Jillian laughed. "That figures. She makes everyone watch that channel."

"That she does. So, how's Nikki doing? Your mom told me all about her little situation."

"She's okay, I guess, but the kids at school won't stop attacking her. They keep saying such hurtful things."

"That's really too bad. Nikki shouldn't have done what she did, but those boys are just as much at fault."

"I know, but nobody's saying anything bad about them. They're all talking bad about Nikki."

"How sad. But you know, Nikki has always been a little on the grown side. She's always been much too fast for her age, and when you're fast like that, boys are quick to take advantage of it."

"I guess."

"It's the truth, and your grandfather and I were just talking yesterday and saying how proud we are of you and how you always carry yourself. You've always been a very caring and obedient child with a good heart, and those are the things that will make life good for you when you get older. Keep your innocence, Jill, until you're old enough to fall in love and get married. Don't ever let anyone take that away from you while you're a child, because it's just not worth it. There's nothing wrong with waiting and nothing wrong with doing exactly what the Bible teaches us to do."

"I know, Grandma," Jillian said, and like every other time when the subject of sex came up, she thought about her father. She thought about all the fondling, all the oral sex he'd made her give him, and even about the naked pictures he'd taken of her against her will. She thought about every single incident and was deeply ashamed of herself.

"So, do you want to speak to Layla?"

"Yes, and then I'll speak to Grandpa."

"Actually, Layla was asking if you were going to spend the night here as well."

"I wish I could but I need to use my computer for my homework. I don't have a lot but it'll still take me a couple of hours or so."

"Oh well, then I guess that's out, because this old thing your grandfather and I have over here is about as slow as a turtle."

"Actually, it's worse than that, Grandma," Jillian said, and they both chuckled.

Jillian chatted with Layla, who still begged her to come spend the night with her, and then Jillian talked with her grandfather. Jillian missed Layla whenever she wasn't at home, and if Layla was going to stay at their grandparents' again tomorrow night, Jillian would have her mom take her there right after school was out. Actually, now that her father was back, and seemingly for good, she wished she and Layla could stay with her grandparents indefinitely.

After another half hour passed, Jillian decided to call Kyle. Yes, her father didn't want her talking to him, but it wasn't like he was going to find out anyway. Right now, he was much too busy begging her mother to forgive him, so who she called on the phone was the very least of his concerns.

"I thought maybe you changed your mind," Kyle said as soon as he answered.

"I was online with Nikki and then I called my grandparents and my little sister."

"Oh. So, what's up with your girl?"

"Not much. But she's already dreading coming to school in the morning, and I don't blame her."

"This whole thing is wack, if you ask me, and Marcus is on a straight rampage. I mean, he treats plenty of girls like dogs, but this is the worst I've ever seen it. And a lot of this is Nikki's fault."

Jillian didn't like the idea of him placing most of the responsibility on her friend. "Why do you say that?"

"Because it was one thing for her to do it

with him the first time he asked her, but to give it up to three dudes all at one time, well, that was just crazy."

Jillian didn't want to talk badly about Nikki, but she couldn't deny how much she agreed with Kyle.

"I just hope all of this dies down soon, because if it doesn't, I'm not sure how Nikki'll be able to handle it. She's so sad and so upset, and she hated being at school today."

"It'll all pass eventually, but with this kind of stuff it's hard to say when. I'm just surprised at how both of you could be best friends for so long and yet be so different."

Jillian defended their relationship. "The reason I'm friends with her is because she's a good person. And I can trust her with my life."

"I guess."

"I'm serious. Nikki would do anything for me, and I would do the same for her. We love each other like sisters."

"And there's nothing wrong with that, but I gotta tell you, I'm glad I started talking to you and not her, because your girl, Nikki, is out there. She's wild, and she's a big liar."

"What did she lie about?"

"Being a virgin. I mean, wasn't she smart enough to know that you can't hide some-thin' like that? Because even when we were leaving practice this afternoon, Marcus was still talking about how easy it was for him to get inside her. He said there was no struggle or tightness at all. Not even a little."

"I don't wanna talk about this anymore," she said, but wondered the same thing she had earlier: Why hadn't Nikki told her about this other boy she'd done it with? They told each other everything . . . well, almost everything. But not once had Nikki ever mentioned having sex before she'd had it with Marcus.

"Fine. Let's talk about us then. Let's talk about when you're going to let me kiss you again."

"I don't know."

"Well, whenever it happens, I hope you like it a lot better than you did the night of the dance, and we definitely have to make sure your dad is nowhere around, because that dude is scary. Maybe we could do it at school."

"Maybe."

"I'll let you know where before lunch."

"Okay. But hey, I'd better go so I can get started on my homework."

"Me too. I'll see you at your locker before first hour, though."

"Talk to you later."

Jillian hung up the phone and pulled out her math book, but to her regret, her father knocked on her door and then came in before she could say anything.

"Your mother just went down to start dinner," he said, closing her door behind him.

Jillian said nothing.

"I know you're probably upset with me so I just wanted to come and tell you how sorry I am. I'm sorry about the terrible mistake I made and I promise you, I'll never cause problems for our family again. I've prayed and asked God to forgive me, and I know He already has."

Jillian still didn't speak.

"I could never take being away from you and Layla, and I can't even imagine what I would do if you and I couldn't spend time together anymore. But thank God, everything is good now, and we'll never have to worry about that. Our lives will be back to normal in no time.

Jillian just stared at him, but he walked closer to where she was sitting and stroked her hair from front to back.

"I love you so, so much."

His voice sounded too serious, and Jillian's nerves raced chaotically. She'd heard him say these words many times before, but today, he spoke in the same way husbands speak to their wives.

"You're so precious and so very special to me," he said, smiling, and Jillian wanted him to leave.

"Byron, honey, can you come down here for a minute?" she heard her mother yelling from downstairs.

Her father looked at her strangely and then moved hastily toward the door and opened it. "Sure, baby. Is something wrong?"

"I need you to come take a look at one of the burners on the stove because it's not lighting up properly."

"I'll be right there," he said, and then turned back to Jillian. "You'd better get back to your schoolwork, and I'll see you downstairs later."

Jillian watched him exit her room and wished he would drop dead.

CHAPTER 19

It was amazing how things could change so drastically in only a three-week period. Jillian's father hadn't made her perform even one sexual deed for him, and she couldn't have been more relieved. She was sure this was all simply a result of his spending every free moment he had with her mother and his behaving as though they were on a second honeymoon, but she was happy nonetheless. Interestingly enough, her mother was happy, too — thrilled was more like it — and she acted as if her husband hadn't even had an affair. She acted as if he'd been completely faithful to her since the very first day she'd met him and like their marriage was perfect.

But not everyone was feeling so blissful. At first, it had seemed as though Nikki was going to be okay, especially since the rumors and ridiculing had ended almost completely after the first week. However, as the days had gone on, Nikki had slipped into what Miss G had described to Jillian's mom as "a severe state of depression" and had taken too many of her mother's sleeping pills. Miss G had found Nikki unconscious in her bedroom, and while Jillian didn't know all the facts, what she did know was that the doctors had been forced to pump her stomach and that she'd been admitted to the hospital. She'd been there for a whole fourteen days now, but Jillian hadn't seen Nikki or spoken to her yet because her doctor didn't want her having too many visitors. The good news, though, was that Miss G had promised Jillian she would pick her up this weekend to go see her, and Jillian couldn't wait. She missed talking to Nikki, and she wanted to be there for her. She wanted to let her know that she was still her best friend and that she would help her in any way she could.

Although that would all depend on whether Jillian got caught doing what she was getting ready to do with Kyle right now. She wasn't sure why she'd let him talk her into slipping outside the school building during their lunch hour, but that's exactly what they'd done only a few minutes ago, and already Jillian was regretting it.

"Why are you acting so nervous?"

"Because. You know we're not supposed to be out here, and if someone finds out about it, we'll be suspended. Plus, it's cold."

"One of my boys is gonna text me as soon as it's safe for us to come back in, so it'll be fine. He'll be texting me in a few minutes, though, so we'd better hurry up."

Jillian braced herself, and Kyle gently eased her body against the light tan brick building. Then he wrapped his arms around her waist and kissed her. She kissed him back and all was well for the first twenty seconds or so, but then her father's face flashed through her mind, live and in vivid color. She saw his face as clearly as if he were standing right in front of her, and she shoved Kyle away from her again, the same as she'd done just a few weeks ago.

Kyle frowned immediately. "Girl, what in the world is wrong with you?"

"Nothing."

"Then, why do you keep doing that?"

"I don't know. I'm sorry."

"Look, Jill, if you don't want to be my girl, then I wish you would just say it and stop playing all these childish games."

"I'm not playing games. I just —"

"Whatever," he said, interrupting her and pulling out his vibrating phone. "That's him, so let's just go before we end up in trouble."

"Now, what are you two doing out here in the middle of the school day?" a tall, wavy-haired officer said in a deep voice.

"Nothing," Kyle lied.

"And what about you, young lady? Were you doing nothing, too?"

"Yes. I mean, no, we were just talking."

"And you couldn't just *talk* in the cafeteria?"

Jillian felt like the entire world was coming to an end — at least her own personal world anyway — especially if her mother was going to be notified about this.

"What are your names?" the officer asked.

"Jillian Maxwell."

"Kyle Davis."

"Mayhorne," the officer called out to one of the other policemen on his two-way pager. "This is Scott. Hey, let Principal Meyers know that I'm on my way in with two truants," he said, and recited both their identities.

Truants? Jillian thought. Was he serious? They were only standing just outside the building and were nowhere near away from school grounds, so what was he talking about?

"Let's go, you two. Now."

Kyle looked just as terrified as she was,

and all she could think was how this was the first time she'd ever been ordered to the principal's office for breaking any rules.

As soon as they walked inside Mrs. Meyers's office, she closed the door and told both of them to have a seat. Officer Scott sat adjacent to them.

"So, what is this all about?" she asked, leaning back in her chair.

Kyle cleared his throat. "We were just talking."

"Okay, but why were you outside when you know you're not supposed to leave from inside the school during lunch or class time?"

"I don't know," he said. "But, Mrs. Meyers, I promise it'll never happen again."

"No, I'm sure it won't. But you do know that the district's latest discipline code states that when a student leaves the building or a classroom without permission, I have the authority to place you on in-school suspension, right?"

"Yes, ma'am."

Jillian nodded her head in agreement as well. She knew all about this brand-new policy, because she'd heard about other kids sneaking out and getting caught in one way or another. She also knew the principal didn't mind suspending people and even expelling them, because after Miss G had reported Marcus and his two friends, Mrs. Meyers had kicked Marcus out of school for ten days for participating in consensual sexual activities during a school-related event and told him he'd be expelled if he did anything else. He'd tried denying the whole thing, claiming Nikki had lied on him, but with all the boasting he'd done to everyone, it hadn't been hard to find kids who were glad to tell what they knew, including Jillian.

Mrs. Meyers continued. "I also have the right to do nothing at all, but just so we make sure the two of you never do something like this again, I want both of you to report to the in-school suspension room first thing tomorrow morning. You'll only be in there for one full day, but I'll also be calling your parents to inform them about it."

Jillian wept silently.

"And one more thing," Mrs. Meyers said. "From the looks of your files, neither of you has been in any trouble before, so that's even more reason why I have to impose at least some sort of discipline. You are both good kids, and we want you to stay that way from now on."

Jillian wept audibly this time. She wept,

because she knew the punishment Mrs. Meyers had just given them would be nothing compared to her mother's.

CHAPTER 20

Jillian rushed inside the house, dropped her shoulder bag and backpack, and went over to the kitchen phone. She scrolled through the Caller ID and to her dismay, Mrs. Meyers had already tried calling her parents. Thankfully, neither of them was home yet, and she had a mind to erase the number from every phone they had and then dial into the voice mail system to delete whatever message her principal had left. For as long as Jillian could remember, her mom hadn't seen a need to give Jillian their system's password, mainly because she didn't think children had any reason to check grown people's messages, but about a year ago, Jillian had overheard her mother and father joking about how silly it was to create a 1-2-3-4 password. They'd said it was so silly no one would ever think to guess it, and that this was precisely the point.

Jillian hurried from phone to phone, deleting her school's number from the various Caller ID screens, dialed into the voice mail system, and then waited to hear Mrs. Meyers's voice. It was the first and only message that played, but strangely enough, the computerized voice didn't say it was a *new* message. Still, Jillian deleted it and breathed a sigh of relief. She hated doing this kind of thing behind her mother's back, but she just couldn't see letting her mother find out about what she'd done earlier today, and she certainly didn't want her knowing about that in-school suspension penalty.

Jillian grabbed a Granny Smith apple from the ceramic fruit bowl on the counter, pulled a bottle of water from the refrigerator, and ran upstairs. Today had turned out to be a lot better than she'd planned on, and now she could relax for a while and then do her homework.

As soon as she stretched across her bed, though, she heard the phone ringing and saw the words "Mitchell Memorial." She smiled when she realized it must be Nikki calling.

"Hello?"

"Hey, Jill."

"Hey, Nik. How are you?"

"Better."

"I'm so glad to hear that."

"I can't talk very long but my doctor said I could make a couple of phone calls today, so you know I placed you at the top of my list."

"I've really missed you."

"I've missed you, too."

"So, when will you get to come home?"

"Maybe in a couple of weeks or so, but I'm not sure."

"Why so long?"

"Because I'm sick."

"What's wrong with you?"

"Jill, I've got some really serious emotional problems, and that's why I've been so depressed. I've been depressed for a really long time, but the reason no one knew was because I learned a long time ago how to make everyone believe I was the happiest girl in the world."

"But why?"

Nikki didn't respond.

"Nik?"

"Yeah, I'm here . . . Jill, there's something I need to tell you. Something I'd never told anyone until I started doing therapy with my doctor and then sharing with the other kids in my group session here at the hospital. It's a special group for kids just like me."

"What do you mean, kids like you?"

Nikki paused again.

212

"Nikki, please tell me what's wrong," Jillian said, afraid and almost in tears.

"Jill, my dad used to touch me in places he shouldn't have. He started doing it when I was only five years old and maybe before that, but that's as far back as I can remember. I remember those times pretty well because I can still see him touching me the day before I went to kindergarten. I remember him telling me that because I was starting school, I was a big girl now and that big girls got to do special things that little girls didn't get to do."

Jillian was mortified and totally shaken. "Oh my God, Nik."

"But, Jill, he did a lot more than that by the time I was eight, and that's why Marcus kept telling everyone I wasn't a virgin. He was telling the truth, but then when he and his teammates blurted out all that stuff in front of you that day your mom came to get me, I just couldn't take it anymore. I was so ashamed. I was sadder than I'd been in a long time, and I just wanted to die. I started thinking about every one of those times my father had made me have sex with him, and it was tearing me apart. I couldn't pretend anymore, and that's why I took those pills."

"I'm so sorry, Nikki. I didn't know."

"My mom didn't know either, but the best

thing she could have done when I was ten was divorce my father. Because when she did, he never got to do that to me again. I always made her think that the reason I never wanted to go visit him was because I was mad at him for leaving us. So she never made me spend time with him, and he never complained about it."

"Is that why you always said he was working whenever I asked about him?"

"Yep. But, Jill, there are so many other kids in my support group who've had the same things happen to them, too, and some are even boys. Our session is for both inpatient and outpatient children. And you know what?"

"What?"

"It really helps to talk about it, and I'm glad my mom finally knows."

"Wow, what did she say?"

"At first she cried a lot, but then she got mad and said I was lying."

"She doesn't believe you?"

"No."

"Why not?"

"Because I didn't tell her about it until now. Then she said that the only reason I took those pills and made up such a big lie about my father was because I was embarrassed about having sex with those three boys. She said I was making up all these lies, just so I wouldn't have to face all those kids at school anymore."

"Gosh, Nik, it must be hard having her be so angry at you."

"It is. It's very hard. But I'm still glad I told her. And, actually, Jill, I would have told her a long time ago, but my father swore she would never believe me. He swore it all the time, and now I know he was right."

Jillian sat thinking about her own father and how his words to her had always been very similar. But mostly she thought about Miss G and how her disbelief in Nikki offered even more proof that there was no use in Jillian telling anyone about anything. Miss G's denial sadly confirmed that Jillian would have to continue letting her father do what he wanted to her.

"Well, I guess my time is almost up," Nikki said. "But you're still coming to see me this weekend, right?"

"Yep. I'm coming with your mom. I mean, she does still come visit you, doesn't she?"

"Yeah, she comes. She doesn't have a whole lot to say, but she still comes to check on me."

"Then I'll see you in a few days."

"See you then. And I love you, Jill."

"I love you, too, Nik."

Jillian heard her best friend hanging up, and she pushed the end button on her cordless and set it down on her bed. A thousand thoughts circulated in her mind, but the one that stood out the most was the fact that not once had Jillian ever suspected that Nikki's father was doing such awful things to her and that he'd been having real sex with her. The whole idea of it was so unsettling, and if having sexual intercourse with her father was the reason Nikki had tried to take her own life, then Jillian had to make sure her father never got a chance to go that far with her. She remembered back to when all the touching and oral sex had made her want to end her life, too, but she also remembered how quickly she'd snapped out of that way of thinking — once she realized her baby sister would be her father's next victim.

Jillian sat looking out of her window in a daze. That is, until she heard her father shouting her name and saw him storming into her room.

"I spoke with your principal about an hour ago."

He was furious, and Jillian wondered how Mrs. Meyers had been able to get in touch with him since the school had never been in the habit of calling parents at work unless there was some sort of an emergency.

"Here I was making my normal afternoon call to check our home voice mail and then I hear this disturbing message from your principal. So, of course, when I called her back she told me everything. She told me all about you and that boy, Kyle."

"We weren't doing anything. And we were only out there for maybe five minutes."

"You had sex with him, didn't you?"

"No, Daddy. I swear."

"I don't believe you."

"But I'm telling you the truth."

"Did you kiss him again?"

"No."

"Jillian, why are you lying?"

"I'm not." She knew she was but she would never admit to him what really happened. Not this time.

"We didn't kiss or do anything else."

"I hate it when you lie like this. Especially when you don't have to. Especially when all I want is the truth."

His voice was a lot calmer, and Jillian didn't know whether to feel relieved or afraid.

"Look, I'm sorry for getting so angry, but I just don't like you sneaking around with this Kyle character. I don't like what I know he's trying to do with you," he said, sitting down on the bed next to Jillian. "But the more I think about it, I'm starting to realize that maybe there's only one way for you to forget about him."

The odd look in his eyes unnerved Jillian, and she wondered what he was talking about.

"I mean, let's face it, you're a beautiful young lady and I guess you're just a lot more curious about sex than I realized. But actually, princess, I totally understand, because now that your little friend, Nikki, has done it, maybe that's why you're wanting to do it as well. Which is fine, but this Kyle character isn't experienced enough for you to be doing something like that with him. All he is is some little punk who would only hurt you, but I could show you just how special lovemaking is really supposed to be."

Jillian's heart pounded so heavily, she could hear it.

"Making love is the kind of thing that should only happen between two people who love each other. People who love each other the way you and I do."

"But, Daddy, I'm not ready for anything like that. I won't be ready for a very long time, and I never wanted to do anything like that with Kyle either."

"You keep saying that, but if that's true, then why is this the second time you've been caught with him? I caught the two of you myself at the dance, and now some police officer caught you this afternoon."

"But we weren't doing anything."

Her father chuckled like they were watching a sitcom. "Look, princess, whether you admit it or not, I know you've been spending a lot of time thinking about sex. You've been wanting to do it ever since Nikki did it with those three boys, haven't you?"

"No. Having sex before you get married is wrong."

"Not necessarily. Not if the two people doing it have a special kind of relationship and really care about each other."

Jillian stood up, stepped toward her open doorway, and considered running out of it. But her father pulled her back onto the bed and held her arm.

"Look. If you make Daddy happy, your little problem at school can just be our little secret and your mother won't ever have to find out about it. We can make each other happy, princess. So come on. Just lie down and relax."

"No," she said, jerking away from him and leaving the bed again. "Stop it."

"I can't believe you're treating me this way

when you were so willing to be with that Kyle. But then, maybe the reason you're acting this way is because you've already had sex with him. Maybe I was right all along."

"I did not! And please get out of my room. Please leave me alone, Daddy."

Her father got up and walked over to where she was standing. "You're really disappointing me, and you know I don't like that. I don't like how ungrateful you're being when I do everything I can for you. I make sure your mom has enough money to buy you anything you want, and this is the thanks I get for it?"

No matter how many filthy and sinful things he'd made her do in the past — no matter how much she knew she had no choice but to continue letting him do them — she would *never* let him crawl into bed with her and force himself inside her. She would never let him violate her that way. So she backed away from him and then out of her room and ran down the staircase.

Her father called after her, but she ignored him and hurried into the kitchen.

He walked in right behind her. "Why are you all of a sudden acting like I'm the enemy? Like you hate me."

"Daddy, why can't you just leave me alone?"

"Because I can't," he said, slowly walking toward her. "I've tried to love just your mom, but I can't help how I feel about you. And before this silly boy came into the picture, you felt the same way about me. I know you did."

Jillian backed into the sink.

"Princess, please just forget about that boy, and I'll get you anything you want. I'll do anything you ask because I just can't stand the thought of you being with him. I told you before how jealous I was of him. I don't want to be, princess, but I can't help myself."

"Daddy, please stop bothering me!" she screamed.

"Okay, okay. I'll leave you alone if you'll just give me a big hug. That's all."

Jillian didn't want to do that either, but if hugging him would free her from this madness, at least for today, then it was worth it.

"Thank you, princess," he said the moment they embraced each other. "Thank you for being so good to Daddy."

Jillian attempted to pull away.

"Just let me hold you a little while longer and then you can go."

Jillian kept her arms around his waist and

at first he just held her, but then she felt
him caressing her back. She didn't like this,
so she tried easing away from him again.
But this time, he lifted her chin away from
his chest and kissed her. He kissed her
frantically and tried forcing his tongue
inside her mouth. Then, he kissed her on
her neck, moving his lips from one side to
the other. She tried pushing him with both
hands, but he wouldn't release her.

"Daddy, please don't. Stop it. You said just
a hug and that you'd let me go after that."

"Come on, princess," he said between
breaths, and squeezed her body even tighter.

"Daddy, I *said,* stop it!"

She pleaded with all her might, but her
father ignored all that she was saying and
slowly stroked her back and forth between
her legs. Jillian squirmed and yelled as loud
as she could. "Oh God, Daddy, please don't
do this!"

Still, he kept on his mission. "You know
you want this, princess. We've both wanted
it for a long time now," he said, sliding his
hand inside her sweat pants and then inside
her underwear.

"Daddy, I'm begging you. Please don't
make me do this!"

Her father pressed her body completely
into the corner of the kitchen countertop

and held the back of her head with one of his hands, all while kissing her up and down her neck in an out-of-control manner. He then used his other hand to unbuckle his belt and unzip his dress pants.

"Why don't you take care of Daddy the way you always do, and then we'll go back upstairs to your bedroom, so we can make love to each other," he said, still kissing her ferociously and gently pressing down on both of her shoulders, trying to get her onto her knees.

Jillian felt like she was having an out-of-body experience. Like she was watching a movie, starring her and her father. It was a strange feeling, the kind she'd never had before and one she couldn't begin to explain if she wanted to. But she continued watching. She watched and before long, she saw herself reaching and then yanking a butcher knife from its wooden holder. She watched and saw the knife plunging deeply into her father's stomach and then saw his body dropping to the floor.

She watched and knew for sure that she must be daydreaming.

CHAPTER 21

After Jillian's mother had dialed 911, the paramedics hadn't wasted any time arriving on the scene and neither had each of the four police officers and two detectives. Every one of them seemed to be assigned to something different, but it was the officer who'd been given the task of picking up the huge knife with gloved hands that Jillian had paid the most attention to. It just didn't seem real, but she knew there was no denying that she had, in fact, stabbed her father as hard as she could. She'd done it without planning to and, for a few moments, without even realizing it, but now she was fully aware of all the key details. She'd stabbed him, he'd fallen to the floor, and her mother had walked in right afterward.

That was hours ago, but Jillian still remembered it the same as if it was happening now.

"Oh my God, what in the world is going

on here?!" her mother yelled hysterically.

"Nothing," her father struggled to say while moaning in great pain. "I was just . . . just showing her what could happen if she didn't leave that Kyle boy alone. She got caught with him outside at school today and had to be escorted by one of the policemen to the principal's office."

"What? But why are your pants and underwear dropped down around your legs like that? Jill, sweetie, what was he trying to do to you?"

"I told you, baby," her father answered, as if he was the one who'd been asked the question. "Nothing."

"Honey, come here," her mother said, reaching out her arms, and Jillian fell into them, bawling.

Her mother held her close and then looked down at her husband. She stared at him, without saying one word, but then finally called for help.

As soon as she hung up the phone, though, Jillian's father snatched the knife from his body and screamed for his natural life. Blood spewed everywhere, but interestingly enough, her mother only watched and never took one step toward him.

"Roxie, baby, can you please help me?" he asked, reaching out one of his hands to her.

"Help me before I bleed to death."

"You're sick, Byron. You're sick and pathetic, and I can't believe I've been so blind. I can't believe you would expose yourself like this to my innocent little child."

"But I haven't done anything wrong. I mean, maybe I went too far trying to scare her about this Kyle boy, but I've never done anything even close to this before now."

"Excuse me?" her mother said. "Byron, you're lying there practically half-naked. So how can you possibly even try to explain something like this?"

"Because not once have I ever approached or touched my princess in the wrong kind of way. Not one time."

"Yes, he has, Mom," Jillian spat out, surprising herself. "He's been making me do all kinds of stuff with him ever since Layla was born, and I wanted to tell you so bad. I wanted to tell you, but he told me you wouldn't believe me. He told me that we were only doing what all fathers and daughters do with each other and that there was nothing wrong with it. And, Mom, that's why I've been so afraid for you to find out. I've been afraid for five whole years."

"Oh, nooooo," her mother said, covering her face and now weeping. "Lord, God, no. Sweetie, I didn't know, and I'm so sorry."

"Baby, she's lying," her father said. "I don't know why, but she is."

"You . . . make . . . me . . . sick," she said, and then kicked him in his side with her sharply-pointed-toe, three-inch heels.

He bellowed loudly, but her mother kicked him again. And again. And again. She kicked and stomped him in his stomach. She kicked him in his head and also in every other spot her foot randomly landed, and while his moans had now become pretty faint and he seemed nearly unconscious, she wouldn't stop. She kicked and stomped him until her shoe finally flew off.

"Sweetie, I need you to go up to your room, okay?" her mother instructed, breathing fast and visibly, but also in a calm and strange sort of way.

"Mom, no, I don't want to," Jillian said, begging to stay right where she was because she knew if she left her mother alone with her father, he would figure out the right kind of lies to tell her and would convince her mother of just how sorry he was. He would tell her everything he thought she wanted to hear, and her mother would forgive him before sundown.

Her mother hugged her for longer than normal. "There's nothing for you to worry about, but I need you to go upstairs now."

Tears fell down Jillian's face, but she did what she was told. However, when she made it to the stairway and heard her mother say, "I'm going to make sure you never hurt either of my daughters ever again," Jillian ran back into the kitchen.

She gasped when she saw her mother kneeling down, picking up the knife, and raising it high above her head.

"Mom, no!" Jillian hollered, and she could tell she'd startled her mother out of some sort of trance. "Mom, please, let's just wait for the police to get here. Please, Mom."

Her mother gazed at her, then looked back down at her husband, then back at her daughter again, and finally dropped the knife onto the floor, sobbing.

Jillian replayed the entire tragedy three different times before her thoughts moved on to the next phase of the evening, which was all the questioning the detective had taken her through. The tall, silver-haired man had wanted to know everything, from what time she'd gotten home from school to what time her father had arrived to how they'd ended up in the kitchen. The detective had made a lot of inquiries, and Jillian's mother had encouraged her to answer all of them and to tell the truth, but Jillian had frozen up when he'd begun asking her about the abuse — such as how long it had been going on, how often it took place in any given week, and what exactly he had made her do with him. They'd wanted to know everything from A to Z, and Jillian hadn't wanted to talk about it. But when she'd seen that there would be no letting up, she'd told them all that they'd wanted to know. About the fondling, about the oral sex, about the photos, and how as of today, her father had decided it was time for them to make love. Jillian could tell how devastated her mother was, partly because she hadn't stopped crying in over an hour, but mostly because of the drained and shattered look on her face. Of course, Jillian had felt the same way, but at the same time, she'd also felt relieved. She was glad that the heavy burden she'd been carrying for so long had been lifted from her.

That is, until the detective had wanted to know who else she'd told about all of this. "Did you tell any of your family members?" he'd asked. "Like maybe your grandparents? Or how about a close friend? Or maybe even a teacher or neighbor?"

Jillian had listened to him but had said nothing because she knew she hadn't told anyone. She knew there were only three people who knew about every single incident — her, her father, and God — so if they needed witnesses to corroborate her story, then she'd known she was in a whole lot of trouble.

But then, as she sat thinking, she remembered something. Her journal. The same journal she'd written in for weeks now — the same journal she never would have started had Mrs. Peterson, her English teacher, not encouraged her to do so.

"Honey, are you okay?" her mother asked, and Jillian's attention returned to the present.

"Yes," she said, sitting up in her bed.

Her mom sat down on the side of it. "I just don't know what else to say, except I'm sorry. I feel so naïve and so bad about not protecting you, because it's a mother's job to protect her children."

"But you didn't know, Mom. You didn't know because Daddy never did any of that stuff when you were home."

"Still. I'll never be able to forgive myself because if I hadn't married him, he never could have hurt you like that. And you never would have had to defend yourself the way you did this afternoon."

"But I didn't mean to hurt Daddy. Honest, I didn't."

"I know, honey."

"Do you think they're going to make me go back to jail?"

"No, and that's why when they took you down to the station this evening, they never even put you in a cell and they let me bail you out right away."

"But I'll still have to go to court, won't I?"

"Yes."

"Mom, I'm so scared, because what if they send me to prison?"

"Your attorney is going to do the best he can for us, and we're just going to pray and believe that God will take care of everything."

Jillian would do just that, the same as always, but then she paused and changed the subject. "Mom, there's something else I need to tell you."

"Honey, what is it?"

"There were a couple of times when Daddy threatened to start having special times with Layla, if I didn't do what he wanted."

Her mother sighed and looked toward the ceiling.

"But I don't think he did. I think he was just saying that to upset me."

"Either way, I'll have to sit Layla down and ask her."

"Are you going to let her come home tomorrow?"

"I think so, and thank God I had already asked your grandparents to pick her up from school again today, because if they hadn't, she would have been with me when I got home."

"I'm glad, too, Mom, because I wouldn't have been able to stand having Layla see what I did."

"None of what happened is your fault, though, sweetie, and don't you ever forget that. No man has any right to do any of those horrible things, and there's not a child on this earth who deserves something like that."

Jillian thought about Nikki and how Nikki had gone through some of the same things she had, but she was too exhausted to tell her mother about any of that tonight.

But there was one other thing she did want to talk about.

"Mom, will Daddy be okay?"

"I don't know."

"If he lives, do you think he'll go to prison for what he did?"

"Definitely. I can promise you that for sure."

Jillian hugged her mom and hoped she was right.

Her mother hugged her back with such intensity that Jillian could barely breathe.

Finally, she released Jillian and looked at her. Then she broke into tears and grabbed Jillian back into her arms again. "Honey, I am so, so sorry I don't know what to do. You and Layla are my life, and just the thought of what Byron did to you makes me wish I'd killed him. I wish I'd killed him when I had the chance."

"But then, Mom, instead of him, you would have been the one to go to prison. And then Layla and I wouldn't have any parents at all."

"You're right, baby. But this is all just so hard to swallow. I'm so hurt and so angry at myself for not seeing what was happening. Right here in my own house."

"But it's going to be okay now," Jillian said, caressing her mother's back. "Layla and I will be safe because Daddy won't be here anymore."

Her mother continued holding her and for the first time in years, Jillian felt at peace and like she finally had a reason to smile again — without faking it.

EPILOGUE

Six Months Later
It has taken a little while, but thank fully, life for Mom, Layla, and me has gotten back to normal. I did end up having to answer to an assault with a deadly weapon charge but shortly after all the testimony, my journal entries, and all the other evidence had been presented from both sides, a very kind and understanding female judge in juvenile court sentenced me to a six-month supervised probation — which ended effective today. She told me how sorry she was that I'd had to experience such significant trauma at the hands of my father and that she was glad I wouldn't have to live through that same trauma again in a full-fledged trial setting. Then, if that wasn't blessing enough, even the prosecutor offered to expunge my record as long as I didn't get into any trouble. I hadn't been exactly sure of what the word "expunge" meant, but my attorney said it meant that from

this day on, there would be no court record outlining what I'd done to my father. My mom was extremely happy about that and so were my grandparents. I was excited about it, too, because the last thing I wanted was for something so awful to follow me into adulthood.

Sadly, though, while everything did turn out pretty well for me, they didn't go so well for my father, who, ironically, didn't have to suffer through an actual trial either but was sentenced to twenty years with no chance of early parole. But in all honesty, he would have gotten a lot more time than that had he not changed his plea of innocence to a guilty one, something he did very quickly when he realized no jury was going to go easy on him. It was one thing for him to have to answer to the four child sexual exploitation charges relating to me, including the one that focused on those naked photos he'd taken, but it was a whole other when that Deanna girl he'd been having the affair with at work had come forward. She'd heard about my father being stabbed and then arrested, and as soon as she'd learned why, she'd contacted my mom and then came over to see us. To Mom's and my surprise, we recognized Deanna as soon as we laid eyes on her — we recognized her because just a little over five years ago and just before Layla was born, "Dee Dee" would sometimes come babysit me when my parents went out to dinner. She was the same Dee Dee who'd gone to our church, and the one my father had sexually molested for more than a year — the one he'd taken advantage of whenever she would finish babysitting and he would give her a ride home. Worse, Daddy had actually gotten her pregnant back then, when she was only thirteen, but then gave her money and convinced her to have an abortion. This, of course, now explained exactly why he'd been in such a hurry for us to leave Mount Shiloh and move on to a new congregation. That was the first church we'd joined, right after he and Mom had gotten married, so I couldn't help wondering if we'd ended up leaving our last church for the same reason. I wondered if maybe there was yet another young girl he might have had sex with, and maybe something bad had resulted from it. What I wondered more than anything, though, was why Dee Dee had started being with Daddy all over again, five years after the fact, and had allowed herself to get pregnant a second time. She was now six months along, and the reason she said she'd sent Mom that letter was because she'd really been hoping Daddy would leave Mom, so she and him could be together. Dee Dee had apologized repeatedly to Mom, but in the end, Mom had told her how she was the one who was sorry for all that Dee Dee had been through as a child.

But regardless of what we might never find out about him, I was just glad that Daddy was gone. As a matter of fact, sometimes I felt such tiny remorse about forcing that knife inside his stomach, I found myself being consumed with shame and guilt — I felt bad for not feeling the kind of sorrow and regret that maybe I should be feeling. I also felt pretty bad for Layla, who missed him terribly, but at least, according to her, he hadn't touched her in private places. That was the good news, and my hope was that she was telling the truth and not trying to hide anything the way I had out of humiliation and fear.

So, all in all, I was doing better than expected and so was Nikki, who I'm happy to say found out she wasn't pregnant and who was finally receiving the kind of love and understanding she needed from her mom. When she got out of the hospital, though, I told her everything about my father, and she gave me more specifics about her situation, too. We talked a lot, and I was also glad to be attending the support group sessions at the hospital with her one night a week and then counseling with my doctor on Thursdays. At first, I hadn't thought I needed any of that, but with everyone at school discovering what I'd done to my father and then talking about it, both in my face and behind my back, just like they'd done to Nikki, I knew therapy was a good thing. It was necessary, and it was also helping me deal with all the flashbacks I kept having — flashbacks relating to the stabbing and those relating to that hideous relationship I'd been in with my father. Sometimes my strongest memories of him appeared so brightly and boldly, I had to frequently remind myself that he could no longer hurt me.

So, yes, therapy was definitely making a huge difference for both Nikki and me, and it was teaching us so many other things as well. Such as why we and so many millions of other kids just don't tell. Why we keep such deep dark secrets to ourselves and pretend nothing bad is happening to us. Why some abused children, as they grow older, react one way and some act completely different — why some girls like Nikki can't wait to have sex with as many boys as possible and why girls like me are so distraught on the inside that the idea of having sex with any boy is enough to make them cringe. Therapy was also teaching us that without proper counseling, some of those same feelings could even follow us into womanhood and end up making our lives completely miserable. This, of course, reminded me of something I'd heard my mother say for years, "Your childhood, good or bad, will affect you for the rest of your life." But then I was also reminded of another saying she had, too. "For everything bad that happens, something good always comes out of it."

For some reason, I truly believe in that saying and will be reciting it to myself, over and over, for as long as I live.

Because if I do, I know I'll have a promising chance at being okay.

I'll have a great chance at being just as happy as the next person.

I'll be able to hold my head high and do everything I can to live my life to the fullest.

AUTHOR'S NOTE

While *A Deep Dark Secret* is a fictional story, childhood sexual abuse is a very serious problem in this country and one we all need to pay a lot more attention to. The statistics are devastating, and just to give you at least somewhat of an idea of how alarming these numbers are, I have listed a few of them below.

- 1 in 4 girls is sexually abused before age 18
- 1 in 6 boys is sexually abused before age 18
- More than 20 percent of children are sexually abused before the age of 8
- Only 10 percent are abused by strangers (meaning the other 90 percent are abused by a close family member right in their own home or by some other family member or person they know and trust)

- Most perpetrators don't molest only one child if they are not reported and stopped
- 30 percent of victims never disclose the experience to *anyone*
- **An estimated 39 million survivors of childhood sexual abuse exist in America today**

Source: www.darkness2light.org

It is true that I do not know firsthand what it is like to experience the exact same situations that Jillian Maxwell experienced, but sadly, I do know what it is like to have an adult touch me inappropriately when I was a child. I also know what it feels like to go years without telling another living soul, so my greatest hope is that this novella will enhance public awareness and that it will encourage all victims, both surviving and current, to finally get the help they need — it is my hope that every person reading this will become much more conscious of what might be happening to children in his or her own household, church, school, and neighborhood.

If you suspect any child is being sexually abused or you would like help in dealing with what may have happened to you during your own childhood, please call 1-866-FOR-LIGHT.

ABOUT THE AUTHOR

Kimberla Lawson Roby is the *New York Times* bestselling author of the acclaimed novels *Love and Lies, Changing Faces, The Best-Kept Secret, Too Much of a Good Thing, A Taste of Reality, Behind Closed Doors, Here and Now, Casting the First Stone,* and *It's a Thin Line.* She lives with her husband in Illinois.